CABO

CABO
BOOK 2

ROBERT WISEHART

ROUGH
EDGES
PRESS

Cabo
Paperback Edition
Copyright © 2025 (As Revised) Robert Wisehart

Rough Edges Press
An Imprint of Wolfpack Publishing
1707 E. Diana Street
Tampa, FL 33610

roughedgespress.com

Paperback ISBN 978-1-68549-667-8
eBook ISBN 978-1-68549-666-1

CABO

CHAPTER 1

IT WAS JUST after midnight when they came for her.

The first guard died at the compound gate, killed quietly from behind with a knife.

The next guard's throat was slit while he was lighting a cigarette. Like the first, he died without a sound.

The third man was shot when he thought that he heard something unusual and walked around to the rear of the mansion to investigate, where he saw two men hustling *Senora* Tolsa past the swimming pool. What he didn't see was the man behind him, the one who shot him in the back of the head, and shot him again when he fell to the ground.

Although the two shots awakened everyone in the compound, the kidnappers were quickly out of a side gate and into a white Toyota Camry parked on a narrow side street where there was no streetlight to illuminate its presence. The automobile disappeared into the warm night before anyone realized that three men were dead and *Senora* Tolsa was missing.

Three minutes later, the Toyota stopped at the entrance to a trailer park and campground a little more than a mile to the east. The kidnappers got out of the car and casually walked into the trailer park as if they belonged there, pausing only to shoot Estaban Hernandez as they passed his office.

For Hernandez, it was just bad luck. You could even say that his work ethic got him killed. The trailer park manager couldn't sleep and, being a conscientious hard-working man, decided to use the quiet time and catch up on some paperwork. Hearing a car pull up, he assumed that he had a late-night customer, Hernandez left his office and stepped outside to the front porch of the small stucco cottage where he lived and worked. Late arrivals were always grateful when he had a space available and Estaban Hernandez was a man who enjoyed being of service.

Seeing several men and one woman get out of the car, Hernandez smiled and asked, *"Quien es?"* One man stepped out in front of the others and put two shots in Hernandez's chest at close range.

As the kidnappers stepped around Hernandez's body and made their way down a dirt road between the lines of trailers, a small boat waited close to the beach at the rear of the trailer park, gently floating on the calm black water of the *bahia*. No one paid any attention to it earlier in the day because it was just one boat among many.

A man who was bigger and taller than the others took *Senora* Tolsa in his arms, waded into the waist-deep water, and easily lifted her over the side and into the boat. Once the rest were safely on board, the boat took off, its running lights dark, and sputtered into the night. It didn't even seem to hurry.

The whole thing took less than fifteen minutes, a very efficient operation.

CHAPTER 2

THE TELEPHONE RANG a few minutes before seven. We'd already been up for more than an hour but the sound still put a knot in my stomach. I learned a long time ago that nobody calls early in the morning or late at night with good news.

"Hello," I said.

"Cruickshank?"

"Yes."

"It's Valencia."

"I didn't do it, I swear," I said. "I'm an innocent man. I have nothing more to say. You'll have to talk to my attorney, the one they call Poncho the Butcher."

"You didn't do it, but you're certainly not an innocent man," he said. "I've called to ask a favor."

That jerked me out of my early morning torpor. Valencia was a captain with the Cabo San Lucas police department, a man who wouldn't ask for a favor unless it was absolutely necessary and even then he wouldn't like it.

"What is it?" I asked.

"Better if I explain in person," he said. "May I come?"

"Sure."

"Now?"

"Okay."

"I will be there in ten minutes," he said.

As I put the cordless phone back in its cradle on the bedside table, Dina came into the bedroom, wearing only the electric toothbrush in her mouth.

"Who on earth was that?" she mumbled, toothpaste froth bubbling on her lips.

"Valencia," I replied. "He wants a favor."

"What kind of favor?"

"I don't know, but he'll be here in a few minutes."

She took the toothbrush out of her mouth, grinned provocatively, and put one hand on her hip.

"Are you suggesting that my attire may not be appropriate to receive a visitor?" she asked.

"I don't want the poor man driven mad with lust," I said.

Dina grinned again and went back into the bathroom, wiggling her fine butt at me on the way.

Dina always took as much time to dress as there was time available. If she had forty-five minutes, it took forty-five minutes. If she had 90 seconds, it took 90 seconds. By the time Valencia arrived she was her usual perfect self in knee-length white shorts, a red sleeveless blouse, and black sandals. Her dark hair was still damp from the shower and glistened in the morning light.

Valencia parked his Chevy Blazer on the gravel drive in front of our house. I heard the crunch of his tires as he drove up and opened the door before he could ring the bell. He was in uniform; dark blue trousers with a knife-edge crease, black shoes glistening with polish, and a light blue long-sleeve shirt with stiff dark-blue epaulets. Valencia was slim, a little above middle height, and easily the best-looking man I'd ever seen. With his dark hair, neat black mustache, and the whitest teeth on the continent, I always felt like a warthog in his presence. He was also a good cop whose resume included a stint at the FBI academy at Quantico and two years in Europe with Interpol. Only an occasional formality of phrasing gave away that English was his second language.

I waited while Dina and Valencia exchanged air kisses. Brewster, our hundred pound black and brown Beauceron, made himself useful by sniffing around Valencia's ankles. As usual, he couldn't decide whether he was a stalwart watchdog or a ninny. And, as usual, the ninny won, especially now that the intruder was actually *in* the house. Our fearless hound edged up, sniffed, barked fiercely, and then nervously scrambled backwards with his belly close to the ground until he was a safe distance away. At that point, he recovered his courage, barked some more, edged back up to Valencia's ankles, and started all over again.

"No wonder that dog is a rare breed," Valencia said, going down on one knee and holding his hand out, trying to make friends with Brewster for probably the fiftieth time. "Who else would want one?"

Dina picked up her car keys from the wicker basket on the table by the front door.

"I've got an early telephone interview with a travel writer from the New York Times so I'm going into the office," she announced. "I'll leave you two *muy macho* characters to fend for yourselves."

I didn't let her go until we'd exchanged something more substantial than an air kiss. Dina had recently opened a public relations business in Cabo San Lucas, with a nice little office downtown in a sprawling complex on Lazaro Cardenas, the street that more or less qualified as Cabo's main drag. Her specialty was getting play in

American and European media for the area's hotels, restaurants, recreation, and general amusements, of which there are many.

Before we moved to Cabo, Dina had a successful PR business in Southern California, which she sold for a ridiculous amount of money that surprised us both. After a year or so of lolling around on the beach, acquiring a golden body, watching a lot of romantic sunsets, learning to scuba dive, and getting in the best shape of her life, she decided to go back to work. She was good at it in California and she was good at it in Mexico. Maybe even better. Taking a break renewed her enthusiasm for the business and her client list was growing almost faster than she wanted it to. This being Mexico, she had a habit of going to work long before almost everyone else, which was probably one of the reasons why she was doing so well.

"Why don't we go out on the deck?" I suggested.

As we walked through the house, I asked, "You want some coffee?"

Valencia shook his head.

"No more today. I've already had too much."

Valencia was tired and it showed. But instead of looking bleary and worn down, it gave him a kind of tragic Heathcliff-on-the-moors, too-sexy-for-my-badge look. The guy could get on my nerves.

Our deck was done in rich Saltillo tile and sat high above the sparkling ocean, with a view that never failed to make me smile. A meandering dirt path led through the brush and scrub on a gentle slope down to the deserted beach. Even this early the warmth of the morning sun radiated off the tile, although it wouldn't be genuinely hot until mid-afternoon. For now, a light morning breeze off the ocean and the shade provided by our big patio umbrella kept it comfortable. Just another day in paradise, as they liked to say in Cabo.

Our house was on the corridor between Cabo San Lucas and San Jose del Cabo, the little towns at the tip of the Baja peninsula known collectively as Los Cabos. It was much closer to Cabo San Lucas and we could see Los Arcos shimmering in the distance. According to the local lore, the Pacific meets the Sea of Cortez next to Los Arcos at Lovers' Beach. That may or may not be true, but it's such a cool landmark that people want it to be true. As popular images go, Los Arcos, a natural rock formation that makes an arch at the end of the Baja Peninsula, is to Los Cabos what the Golden Gate Bridge is to San Francisco, the Eiffel Tower to Paris, and the Statue of Liberty to New York City, only it isn't man made.

The house nearest to ours was hidden from view a couple of hundred yards down the beach, so the two of us were about as private as we could get.

We settled into wicker chairs separated by a bistro table.

"So what's going on?" I asked.

"Do you know Jorge Tolsa?"

"I've never met him, but I know who he is," I replied. "Everybody knows who he is. You can't be in Cabo for ten minutes without running into something he owns or somebody who works for him. I think Dina's met him a couple of times. She already knows almost everybody worth knowing around here."

Jorge Tolsa's Hotel Sol was one of Cabo San Lucas' first major hotels. It was built back in the early 1950s, when Cabo was just a tiny hard-to-get-to fishing village, and renovated many times since then. At about the same time, Tolsa scraped together everything he owned and bought more than a mile of empty beachfront property for the equivalent of fifteen thousand dollars, a big gamble at the time. Over the years, he parlayed that into four or five more hotels, several restaurants, and a whole lot more beachfront property, some of the most prime real estate in the world. He was heavily into the timeshare business, too. I was pretty sure that wasn't the extent of his holdings, but that was all I knew about.

"Someone kidnapped his wife last night and killed four people doing it," Valencia said.

That one knocked me back in the chair. Despite its raffish reputation and colorful history, which is part of what Dina and I like about it, Los Cabos is not a violent place. The story goes that Hernan Cortez's navigator, a man named Francisco de Ulloa, discovered what would become Cabo San Lucas in 1537. For most of its early history it was a stopover for the English pirates and privateers who had the usual lusty hopes of capturing one of the Manila galleons bound from the Philippines for Acapulco, where they traded porcelain, silk, tapestries, gunpowder and many other products from Asia. When one galleon was captured off the coast by Sir Thomas Cavendish in 1587, in an attempt to rid the waters of such "undesirables" Spain built a small fortress at Cabo San Lucas. It probably seemed like a good idea at the time, but it didn't take. Undesirables, like cockroaches, are always with us. While the fort did help open the area to exploration, the undesirables kept coming, especially after pearls were discovered in the Sea of Cortez. In 1730, a Jesuit mission, San Jose del Cabo, was established on the other side of the peninsula from Cabo San Lucas. After that, life continued pretty much unchanged until the early 1950s, when word got around among the Hollywood swells that Los Cabos offered some of the best sports fishing in the world, everything from marlin and Dorado to Tuna and Wahoo. Bing Crosby, Phil Harris, Desi Arnaz, and John Wayne, among other high rollers, kicked in to build a little hotel so they'd have a decent place to stay when they came down to fish, eat, drink, and be manly. More hotels came after that, Tolsa's Hotel Sol among them.

Even with those changes, the little town didn't really start to boom until the mid-1970s, when the government finally finished the long-awaited peninsular highway that ran the entire sun-baked thousand miles of the Baja Peninsula. Once the highway helped open Los Cabos to the rest of the world, Fonatur, the Mexican government-funded tourist agency, began working with developers to pour money and resources into the area. It wasn't long before Cabo boasted an international airport that seemed to get expanded every six months, a three-hundred slip marina, and big resort hotels springing up all over the place. Condos, resorts, and time shares crawled up the coast on both sides of the peninsula, too. Business boomed so much that even the people who made it boom seemed a little shocked by it all. It's true that whenever the American economy sagged Cabo sagged a little, too, because so much of the money came from America and Americans. But it never lasted long and always came back stronger than before.

The worst problems for the Cabo police usually involved drunken tourists who do the usual stupid things that people who've had too much to drink do everywhere, plus a little petty theft, usually from the drunken tourists. Virtually none of the violence and drug-related nightmares that plague so many of the large urban areas of Mexico, and the United States, too, for that matter, touched Los Cabos, which still seems pretty isolated from the rest of the country. That was another thing we liked about it.

"How'd it happen?" I asked.

"Several men, probably five or six, we think, killed the

guard at the Tolsa compound gate," Valencia answered. "Do you know the place?"

I nodded. I'd never been inside but I passed it often. The house, which couldn't be seen from the street, was surrounded by a ten-foot wall of stucco over cinder block with rolled razor wire on top of the wall. From the outside, the place looked like a fortress. Not long after we moved here somebody told me that Tolsa built the wall many years ago, back when kidnapping for cash practically was Mexico's national sport. Some claimed that it still was. The modest main entrance was on Marina Boulevard, on the other side of downtown Cabo from where we lived. Access was controlled by an armed guard in a gate house and I assumed that there were more guards inside the walls. All told, a charming place to live.

And from what Valencia said, last night all that protection still wasn't good enough.

"They killed the man in the gate house with a knife," Valencia continued. "We assume one man distracted him while another took him from behind. They got inside the house, although there was no sign of forced entry, dragged Maria Tolsa out of her bed, and left the same way they came in, killing two more guards in the process. They had a car waiting nearby and drove a short distance to *El Campeador* trailer park. Do you know it?"

"Uh-huh." I nodded again. "A little this side of town. Maybe a mile or a little more from Tolsa's place."

"They left the car on the street and walked into the park," he said. "It's really more of a campground than a trailer park. Except for the manager, I don't think anyone there is permanent. It's all tourists. Some stay for a few days, others for months."

The sun was getting brighter and warmer as it reflected off the blue ocean. After rubbing his bloodshot eyes with his forefinger and thumb, Valencia took a pair of aviator sunglasses out of his shirt pocket and slipped them on.

"They shot the manager on the steps of his own front porch." Valencia held up two fingers. "Two shots. He couldn't sleep and was doing some paper work when he heard someone drive up. Late-night arrivals there aren't unusual and he thought nothing of it. The backside of *El Campeador* is on the beach, where the kidnappers had a boat waiting. From there, they disappeared. From start to finish, the whole thing probably took less than a half hour."

"How do you know about the boat?" I asked.

"The manager watched them go and heard the boat," Valencia replied. "He told us everything he could before he died at the hospital."

"That's a professional job," I said. "Maybe a little bloody, but professional."

"Exactly," Valencia agreed. "It was fast, efficient, and ruthless. They killed whoever got in their way and never stopped moving."

"Why leave through the trailer park?"

"Once again, they knew what they were doing," Valencia explained. "A water escape route is anonymous, or close to it. But most of the easy water access here is too public. It passes through hotels, resorts, nightlife areas, the marina, and places such as that. The *El Campeador* people are an older and less affluent crowd. They are not so inclined to the nightlife. They get up early and go to bed early. With luck, no one would see the kidnappers and their victim pass. It was just bad luck that the manager happened to be awake."

"Bad luck for the manager, anyway," I said. "What about the boat? Big? Small?"

"Fairly small, we think," he replied. "From the

description of a boat that was there in the late afternoon and wasn't there this morning, it sounds like perhaps sixteen feet with no cabin."

"With so many people on board it must have been riding pretty low, so it couldn't get very far very fast," I said. "That means probably not over to Mazatlan, or anything, though the water was pretty calm last night."

"No, but there are no reports of a boat like it putting in anywhere nearby either, though that doesn't mean it didn't," Valencia said. "There are many possibilities. Once they were out of sight, they could have transferred to a larger boat."

"Or maybe they put ashore on a beach somewhere up the coast and sank the boat?' I added.

"Or they put ashore, left one or two men to get away with the boat and the rest could be anywhere by now," he said.

"Any prints?"

"We identified Maria Tolsa's palm and finger prints on the dashboard of the car, as if she put a hand there to steady herself," Valencia replied. "The position of the print and some hairs we found that match hers indicate that she was sitting in the front on the passenger's side by the door. There are other prints, but the *El Campeador* manager said that the man who shot him was wearing gloves. Since this was so professionally done, I suspect that we won't find any more prints that matter."

"Except from whoever owns the car," I said. "I assume it was stolen."

Valencia gave a rolling motion of his shoulders that I took for assent.

"So where was the husband when his wife was dragged out of her own bed?" I asked.

"Tolsa was in Mexico City on business," Valencia

replied. "He came back in his private jet as soon as he was informed of what happened."

"He must be raising holy hell with all of his friends in high places," I said. "Any ransom note? Any leads at all?"

"No and no," Valencia replied. "As you said, the car, a six-year-old Toyota Camry, was stolen in Los Angeles three weeks ago. No one saw anything at the Tolsa compound, at least no one who is still alive. The manager told us what happened at *El Campeador*, but he wasn't able to provide a helpful description. We didn't get to him until it was too late and he was dying as he talked to us."

Valencia paused to see if I had anything to say.

I knew that Jorge Tolsa was in his seventies. If his wife was about the same age, that might be significant. Older people often have medical problems that either require regular treatment or a particular medication. That might turn into a lead if the kidnappers bought the medication somewhere in order to keep their meal ticket alive.

But I stifled the question before I asked it. If Maria Tolsa had any such problems Valencia already knew about them. I'd already asked too many obvious questions. Any more would be insulting. Valencia knew his stuff.

He didn't seem to notice my hesitation. Judging by the distracted look on his face, Valencia's thoughts were going full speed in fifty directions at once.

"Most of the people staying at *El Campeador* are Anglos who drive their trailers and recreational vehicles a thousand miles down the Trans-Peninsula Highway to get here, and who knows how far before that," he said, breaking the silence. "Like all tourists, they come to fish, to see the sights, to golf, perhaps to dive, watch the whales, and escape winter at home. At best they become uneasy, and at worst frightened, when my men show up to talk to them. They are in a foreign country and feel vulnerable when a police officer appears at their door and starts asking questions about a violent crime. They've also heard too many horror stories about Mexican police, Mexican justice, and Mexican jails."

"Of course, none of those stories could possibly have an iota of truth," I joked.

He ignored me. Valencia wasn't in the mood for my humor, or any humor at all.

"I would appreciate it if you would interview as many of these people as you can to see if anyone saw or heard anything that might help us," he explained. "I think they will feel more comfortable with an Anglo. If they're at ease, they might remember something. We've already talked to a few, but came up with nothing."

"Maybe there isn't anything to find?" I said. "Besides, it's been a while since I did this kind of work. You know that."

"True, but you are a private detective," he said. "You know what we're looking for and you know how to get it if it's there. That's all we need."

I couldn't see Valencia's eyes behind the sunglasses. It seemed to give him an advantage. I didn't know why I felt that way. He wasn't looking for an advantage. It wasn't that kind of conversation. But I did anyway. It probably had something to do with my guilty conscience.

"I owe you," I said. "You know that."

A shadow of displeasure crossed Valencia's face as he made a dismissive waving gesture.

"You owe me nothing," he said. "If you don't want to do this, I understand. It's a considerable imposition and may not lead to anything useful."

I didn't say anything. I wasn't thinking about Valencia's request as much as I was just letting it lie there, like I was waiting for an epiphany, or for the clouds to part.

But epiphanies are rare, and there weren't any clouds this morning.

I shrugged. "Oh, hell. Why not? It's not like my social calendar is all that crowded. I assume you'd like me to get started as soon as possible?"

"Now would be good."

Valencia pushed himself out of the chair.

"By the way, there is no money to pay for your time."

"Now there's a surprise," I said.

CHAPTER 3

DESPITE ITS GRAND NAME, *El Campeador* didn't look like much from the outside. Although I'd driven past it practically every day since we moved to Cabo, I'd never been inside.

Following Valencia's SUV, I parked my 1965 Mustang on the street and Valencia led me through the police cordon. I ducked under the yellow crime scene tape stretched across the entrance and entered the trailer park. Before doing anything else, I wanted to get familiar with the layout.

It turned out that *El Campeador* didn't look like much from the inside either. Two narrow streets of hard-packed dirt ran from the entrance all the way back to the *bahia*, with two short cross streets to link them. The cross streets weren't much more than dirt paths barely wide enough for a vehicle to pass. In the center of the complex there was a small unpainted cinder-block building with a marginally clean unisex bathroom and a washer and dryer operated by tokens. A sign on the wall of the laundry room in Spanish and English said that tokens could be purchased at the office. I hadn't been to a coin laundry in years and it cost a lot more than I remembered. Next to the building there was a rusty swing set and a dilapidated wooden see-saw that looked kind of sad. They had not only seen better days, but those better days full of the joyous cries and laughter of children were an awfully long time ago.

In short, the place wasn't particularly attractive. In fact, it was downright ugly. But *El Campeador* was undeniably popular. Out of probably a hundred spaces or more I only saw four vacancies. Judging by the license tags, everyone was from somewhere else. Most of them were from the United States, especially California and Arizona, along with a handful of Canadians who drove a hell of a long way to get here. If I lived in the frozen foods section of the world, I'd probably drive a long way for warm weather, too. There were splendid motor homes, enormous apartments on wheels worth hundreds of thousands of dollars; several Airstreams, those silver retro-looking trailers with rounded corners that I always kind of liked; a bunch of Winnebagos; fancy trailers with extensions that went up and/or sideways; a few pop-up trailers; a couple of old-fashioned Volkswagen campers, the kind that were so popular in the joint-smoking '60s; and just about everything else that was big enough to sleep in and still get you down the road.

I started with the camper closest to the office. It took about 90 minutes for me to reach the conclusion that either nobody saw anything, or they wouldn't admit it if they did. One problem was that most people don't know gunfire when they hear it so the shots didn't get their attention. Conditioned by movies and television, they expect a loud noise when the real thing sounds more like a pop, especially if it's heard from a distance. If Valencia was right about the clientele, most of the people in *El*

Campeador probably slept right through the shots. I talked to three people who said that they thought they heard shots, or something that *might* have been shots, but they were groggy from sleep. They decided that they hadn't really heard anything, rolled over, and went back to sleep. A retired IBM engineer and Vietnam War veteran who wore a t-shirt that declared him to be the World's Greatest Grandpa was positive that he heard two shots, but when he looked out the window of his Winnebago he didn't see anything suspicious. He wasn't sure if the shots came from inside the campground either. Sound does funny things, especially when it's close to a large body of water.

"I *know* there were shots, though," he said. "Two of them. I heard enough of it in 'nam to know gunfire when I hear it."

Since I already knew there were two shots, nothing he told me was very helpful, and I thanked him for his time.

Although by now I was pretty sure that I was wasting my day, I kept plugging away. It took three hours to get down one side of the first street. It would have taken even longer, except that nobody was home in several of the trailers. I'd come back and take care of those later. At this rate, I could probably turn this thing into a career, except I don't think you can have a career if you don't get paid. In that case, it would be more of a hobby, like collecting stamps or watching birds. The day was getting hot, too. I could feel my shirt sticking to my back.

And then, on the other side of the street, my luck turned.

I knocked on the door of a big trailer with a pale green canvass awning that extended out over a cement slab and turned it into a nicely shaded patio. It wasn't beautiful, but it got the job done. In Cabo San Lucas, shade is a really good idea, especially in the summer. There was a small redwood picnic table and two cheap aluminum frame chairs on the patio. The trailer had probably been maneuvered into the slot by the dark blue Dodge Ram pickup parked alongside. With its Cummins diesel, the truck could have pulled the Queen Mary.

The door was opened by a woman who looked to be in her mid-thirties, with shoulder length brown hair gathered at the nape of her neck by what I recently learned was called a scrunchy. Her light-gray shorts came to mid-thigh and contrasted nicely with her tanned legs. The sleeves of her dark-blue blouse were rolled up to just above her elbows. She had a silver bracelet on one wrist and a silver Seiko watch on the other. Her longish face was friendly but challenging at the same time. She was kept from being beautiful by a nose that was a little too small for her face, but I thought that instead of detracting from her looks, it gave her character.

I tried not to be obvious while I checked her out. I had the feeling that she was doing the same thing. I resisted the temptation to suck in my gut. Sooner or later, I'd have to let it go.

I explained what I was doing and why I was doing it.

"Got any ID?" she asked.

I showed her my driver's license, along with my private investigator's license from California.

"This is from California," she said. "Any way you can prove you're really working for the local police?"

She was the first one to ask that question. The others I talked to happily chattered away without any proof that I really was who I said I was. Sharp and good looking, too. Not bad.

"Feel free to call the Cabo police department and ask for Captain Valencia," I said. "He'll vouch for me."

"Wait here," she said, closing the door.

Having nothing better to do, I did what I was told.

She was back in three minutes, although it seemed like a lot longer. When you're waiting outside on a hot day, it always does.

"Okay, you check out," she said. "What do you want to know?"

I gave her the Reader's Digest version of what happened last night and asked if she saw or heard anything out of the ordinary, or anything at all, for that matter, even if it seemed ordinary. Maybe she saw somebody getting in or out of the boat yesterday? Or noticed somebody hanging around earlier in the day?

"Even if it seems insignificant to you, it might help," I said. "You never know."

"Yeah, I know the drill," she said.

She stared at me for a long time. I didn't want to be the first to break the silence, but she out-waited me. It was too hot to dawdle.

I crossed my fingers and held them in the air.

"Scout's honor," I said. "I have not come here to cause you any trouble. Nobody wants to do that. The situation is exactly as I explained it. The police will be grateful and so will I. For one thing, it's hot out here. If you didn't hear or see anything, I'll move on. But if you've got something, or think you do, let's talk about it."

She looked at me for a while longer and seemed to make up her mind about something.

"Wait here again," she said. "I'll be back in just a minute."

She shut the door and I waited some more. I heard voices from inside the trailer. It sounded like an argument. If it was, at least it was short. This time, she returned with another woman. They stood in the doorway, shoulder to shoulder, and I looked up at them. The new one was taller, probably close to six feet. She was bigger all over, too. The word husky came to mind, although she was more attractive than the word implies. Her hair was shorter than mine and blond. Her face and nose were red from too much sun. She had a broad face with prominent cheekbones and crisp blue eyes. Just now they were troubled eyes, too. As she stood in the doorway, everything from her defensive posture to the wary look on her face sent the message that she was not happy to see me.

"This is Lilly," the first one said.

I nodded, offered my hand, and she took it in a firm grip.

"Hi, Lilly," I said, brilliantly as ever.

"And you are?"

"My name is Ethan Cruickshank. Did your friend here – I turned to the first one; "I'm sorry but I didn't get your name" – tell you what I'm doing?"

I didn't get her name because she didn't give it. But I didn't want to be so obvious as to point that out. Subtle is my middle name.

The first one smiled a little. She got my point. I was making progress.

"My name's Nicole," she said.

"Lilly and Nicole," I said, nodding at each one as I said their names. "Okay."

Maybe it was possible to sound more inane but I doubted it. I don't think this was what Valencia had in mind when he asked for the help of Ethan Cruickshank, master interrogator.

"Come inside and we'll talk," Lilly said.

There was still some hesitation there; a reluctance that seemed more substantial than what I'd encountered with the others I'd talked to. I tried to put them at ease.

"It's a nice day," I said. "If you'd rather do this outside it's …"

"No," Nicole said firmly. "For what we have to tell you inside is better."

They backed away from the door to let me in. I trudged up three metal steps and stepped through the doorway into the trailer, or camper, or whatever it was.

Inside would be better. Nicole promised.

CHAPTER 4

THE INSIDE of the trailer was nicer than many homes and apartments I'd seen, including some of my own back when I was single. Through an open door at one end I could see an unmade queen bed. Next to the bedroom was a door that I assumed led to the toilet, which was across from another door that probably opened to a shower.

Nicole and Lilly guided me to the other end of the trailer and motioned toward one of two identical white leather chairs separated by a lamp table. I took that as an indication that I should sit down, so I did. Along the way, we passed through the tiny kitchen, a dinette, and a sofa bed against one wall. The sofa bed was tucked into in a slide-out extension that ran along the side of the trailer opposite the entrance. When the trailer was on the road and the extension pushed in, the sofa bed probably covered most of the floor space. The sensation was of being in an over-furnished studio apartment that was a lot longer than it was wide.

Lilly sat in the companion chair next to mine while Nicole eased onto a stool at the kitchen counter. My first impression was confirmed. Nicole had nice legs. I couldn't tell about Lilly's. She was wearing white pants, sandals, and a white blouse with no sleeves.

"As you've probably figured out by now, we have something to tell you," Nicole explained. "The thing is, we're not quite sure how to go about it."

"Why don't you just start and see how it goes?" I suggested. "I repeat; there's no trouble in this for you. None at all."

With my eyes bouncing from Nicole to Lilly and back, I probably looked like the shiftiest character in Mexico, not exactly someone to inspire trust. Nevertheless, I babbled on.

"The police need some help with this thing. It's routine to talk to everybody here and most of them are Anglos. I live in Cabo and I'm friends with the captain. I've had a little experience in this line, so he asked me to help. He figured that a uniformed officer might make people nervous, and he's probably right. There's the language problem, too. It's easy for detail to get lost in mangled language. Anything you can tell us - them, I mean - will be much appreciated."

I was selling like crazy. Maybe they'd buy it and maybe they wouldn't, but at least I could take pride in a professional effort.

Nicole looked at Lilly and raised her eyebrows as if to ask an unspoken question. In response, Lilly took a deep breath and let it out with a mighty expulsion of air.

"I saw them,' she said.

"How do you mean?" I asked, my hopes rising. "Saw who?"

"I saw them last night," she said. "I saw them shoot the manager, go through the park, and get in a boat."

I looked hard at Lilly. She looked back.

"I'd say that's pretty interesting," I said. "Tell me exactly what happened."

CHAPTER 5

"It was after midnight, maybe twelve thirty, or so," Lilly said. "I couldn't sleep and went outside for a smoke."

"I won't let her smoke inside," Nicole interrupted.

"I was sitting at the table when I saw the manager walk out of his place over there." Lilly motioned in the direction of the manager's office. "There was a group coming in from the street and the manager came out to see what they wanted, I guess. It looked like maybe a half-dozen, though I didn't count. The woman must have been in the middle because with all the men around her I didn't see her until later. The manager said something, but it was too far away to hear it. You know how it is; I heard his voice, but not the words. One guy stepped out in front of the others. He made a kind of casual waving motion with his left hand, like he was saying hello. At the same time, he pulled a weapon with his right, fired two rounds and put the manager down."

Lilly stopped, leaned back in the chair and stretched her legs out. Then she looked up at the ceiling and closed her eyes, replaying everything in her mind's eye.

"I was stunned for a second, you know? It's not something you see everyday. Then I ran inside to get my gun.

It was all impulse. I didn't stop to think it through. There wasn't time. I just did it. For all I knew, these guys, whoever they were, intended to shoot their way through the park. I know that sounds kind of dumb now, but that's the way I felt. My adrenalin was pumping like crazy."

"What kind of gun?" I asked.

"What do you mean what kind of gun?" she asked. "Me or the shooter?"

"You," I said. "I assume you were too far away to see his weapon."

"What does that have to do with anything?" she snapped.

Lilly was edgy and it showed. She still wasn't sure that she was doing the right thing by talking to me.

"Probably nothing at all." I used my most soothing voice, the one that can even put me to sleep. "It's just another detail. You accumulate all the detail you can and see where it takes you. Sometimes it doesn't take you anywhere, but sometimes it does. You ask questions because that's what you do, even if they seem dumb or pointless."

Lilly thought about that and decided it was okay.

"It's a Sig Saur nine with a ten-shot magazine," she said. "And yeah, I was too far away to ID the shooter's weapon."

Her answer - really more the way she answered - established that she knew guns, which was why I asked the question.

"We both have one," Nicole added.

I wanted to ask why but decided it could wait. It was best to let Lilly continue with her story.

"Go on," I said.

"They couldn't see me," she continued. "My pajamas are black and the street light" – she nodded through the window – "is out. I think most of 'em are out. The maintenance budget for this place must be like ten bucks a year. It's pretty dark at night."

I nodded. It was a friendly nod, a small gesture of encouragement from their old pal Ethan; their old pal they met about ten minutes ago and who was drawing them into something they obviously didn't want.

"I was gonna take a shot at 'em," Lilly said. "I got down on one knee and aimed across the picnic table. The shooter still had his gun out and he was walking a little ahead of the others. When they were close enough I was gonna let go."

"Where were they when you were getting ready to shoot?" I asked.

She pointed. "In the middle of the road out there. Like I said, that's what I was *gonna* do, but Nikky stopped me."

I turned to Nicole.

"You stopped her?"

"Hell, yes, I stopped her! She woke me up when she came inside to get her piece. I couldn't figure out what she was up to, so I got up and followed her to the door. When I saw her aim across the table, I went outside and grabbed her."

"What happened then?"

"We were kneeling by the table and she told me what happened," Nicole said. "We watched 'em as they passed by and that's when we saw the woman."

"They were headed down the road to the beach," Lilly said. "Nikky's right. I should have stayed out of it. What was I gonna do, shoot 'em all? Like I said, it was impulse. I didn't have a thought in my head."

Lilly looked sheepish and a little embarrassed. So far, this was not a particularly flattering story and I gave her major points for telling it.

"Anyway, they went on down to the beach, waded into the water, and got in a boat," she continued. "There was at least one guy in the boat waiting. We followed so we could see what was going on, but kept at a distance so they couldn't see us."

"You're sure they never spotted you, or heard you when Nicole kept you from shooting?" I asked.

Both of them shook their heads.

"We're positive," Lilly said. "It was dark, and we stayed pretty far back. I didn't even see any of 'em look back this way. They seemed pretty sure of themselves. Almost cocky, from their body language."

Lilly and Nicole didn't know any more. Considering the darkness, their descriptions weren't bad, although it was mostly general observations about height, weight and clothing. Nicole remembered that the kidnapper who seemed to be giving the orders had a beard and was taller than the rest, a bigger man all around. He wasn't the one who shot the manager, but he was the one who lifted the woman into the boat. They had nothing much to say about the boat, which slowly disappeared into the night, riding low in the water, a boat like any other boat.

"There is one other thing," Lilly said.

"What's that?"

"I could swear that I heard a shot from the boat a little while after they left, or at least from somewhere out that way," she said. "The sound was real faint and by then we couldn't even see it. It didn't have lights on, or anything. But I'm sure I heard a shot."

For confirmation, she looked at Nicole, who vigorously nodded her agreement.

"Do you mind if we go outside so you can walk me through everything you saw?" I asked.

With Lilly leading, we left the trailer, walked down the metal steps, across the patio, and out to the dirt road toward the office. The two cops Valencia stationed at the *El Campeador* entrance pretended to ignore us, though I could feel their attention.

"They were right here when they shot the manager," Lilly said, stopping in front of the sad little cottage. "He went down over there by the steps."

She led us down the dirt road toward the beach.

"They were right about here when I came out of the trailer with my gun."

"You were lucky I saw what you were doing," Nicole scolded. "You could have shot some innocent camper in his sleep. You're so irresponsible sometimes I can't believe it."

Lilly looked miffed, although she didn't reply. Nicole was right, but Lilly didn't like being reminded of it. I had the feeling that arguing was second nature for these two. It probably was an important part of their relationship, whatever it was.

I left the dynamic duo and walked down to the beach. They followed, still arguing.

"What was I supposed to do, nothing?" Lilly asked.

"Nothing would have been better than what you tried to do and you know it." Nicole wasn't cutting Lilly any slack. "You're just too stubborn to admit it. We could have been in real trouble."

Intrepid soul that I am, I stayed out of it.

The white sandy beach wasn't particularly deep. At high tide it was no more than thirty yards from the campground to the water's edge. A couple of sunbathers were lounging on a beach blanket, with a Styrofoam cooler at their side. Like the police earlier, they tried not to be obvious while they eyeballed us.

"How far out was the boat?" I asked.

"Not far," Lilly replied. "Maybe forty yards, maybe a little less. They were only in waist-deep water when they got in. The big guy lifted the woman into the boat like she weighed nothing at all."

"How was she?" I asked. "Did she seem hurt, or anything?"

Lilly shook her head.

"As far as I could tell she was walking right along with them. She wasn't hurt that I could tell. I didn't see her fight or try to resist, if that's what you're asking."

"She didn't have a hell of a lot of choice," I said, thinking out loud. "What would have been the point of fighting a half-dozen men who'd just killed four people? The best she could hope for is that they wouldn't hurt her. Struggling wouldn't get her anywhere and it seems like she was smart enough to know it."

"Or maybe she was too scared to try," Nicole added.

We walked back to their trailer and climbed in to resume our earlier positions.

"I was asleep, right over there," Nicole said, pointing to the sofa bed. "Lilly sleeps in the bed."

They must have seen something on my face.

"No, we don't sleep together," Lilly said. "Sooner or later, people always wonder about that, even if it's none of their business. The thing is, we're not lesbians." She hesitated. "Well, Nikky's not."

It seemed best to ignore that revelation. It didn't matter anyway. For all I cared they could fondle sheep.

"What are you two doing armed?" I asked. "Unless you're hunting, and a Sig nine isn't anybody's idea of a hunting weapon, Mexico's awfully touchy about that kind of thing. You're breaking about ten kinds of laws by bringing guns across the border. If you got caught, the authorities would not treat you with kindness."

An alarm went off in my head, the one that warned me when I sounded like a nincompoop, although I didn't always listen to it. "The authorities?" Where the hell did that come from? I must be channeling Sydney Greenstreet.

Nicole and Lilly looked at each other; then at me.

"The thing is, we're PIs back home," Nicole said.

"So we're familiar with firearms," Lilly added. "Besides, you know how it is for women on the road; for anybody, really. You can't be too careful."

She had a point, even if she was still wrong. Bringing guns into Mexico was a bad idea. But what did I care? Not for the first time today, I asked myself what I was doing here. What started as a favor to a friend had turned into further proof that no good deed goes unpunished. I promised myself to cut down on good deeds in the future.

"So how much trouble do you think we're in when the cops find out?" Nicole asked.

"About the gun thing? Despite what I said, not much. Actually none at all is my guess. It might be different at another time. If you got caught carrying you'd be up to your necks in it. But the local police have a few other things to think about just now. Besides, remember what I said earlier; you're doing them a favor. They're not gonna replay you by throwing you in the pokey, not even in Mexico."

"Dammit, Nikky, now I kind of wish you hadn't stopped me," Lilly said.

I let them argue. I was thinking about the third shot, if that's what it was. Maybe they only thought they heard it? Like Lilly said, their adrenalin was pumping. Under the circumstances they might have thought they heard almost anything. And even if they did hear something, that didn't necessarily mean it was a shot. Do boat engines backfire? I didn't have the faintest idea.

Besides, it wasn't any of my business, was it? I'd done my good deed for the day.

CHAPTER 6

I TOLD Nicole and Lilly they'd have to tell Valencia everything they told me, emphasizing once again that they weren't in any trouble, although Valencia probably would confiscate their weapons.

"Do you think we need a lawyer?" Nicole asked. "We could call ours back home. He's pretty good, though I don't know how much he knows about Mexican law."

"Call him if it makes you more comfortable, but for what it's worth I don't think it'll be necessary," I said. "It might even make it worse. Lawyers have their uses, but they also have a way of making things more complicated than they have to be. Valencia wants your information; he doesn't want you. You can trust him. I do. There is one sure thing, though. I don't know what your plans are, but he won't want you to leave Cabo for a while. Other than the woman who was kidnapped, you two seem to be the only people left alive who saw the kidnappers."

Other than a quick exchange of glances, they didn't react to the prospect of having to stay in Cabo for an indefinite period. Maybe they were planning to hang around for a while anyway? For all I knew, they just got here and intended to spend the next six months luxuriating on the beautiful grounds of *El Campeador*. Lucky them.

I left their trailer, walked out to my Mustang, and called Valencia. I gave him the highlights of what Nicole and Lilly told me and said they were expecting him.

"I'm on my way," he said.

When Valencia barreled up in his Blazer seven minutes later, I led him to the trailer and introduced him to Lilly and Nicole before plunging back into my exciting door-to-door canvass of *El Campeador*.

It took the rest of the day. I promised myself to come back later tonight or tomorrow to get those I missed, although I didn't think it would do much good. No one else I talked to saw or heard anything. Or, if they did, they didn't admit it.

Feeling hot, tired and grumpy, I drove home, grabbed a can of Tecate from the refrigerator, took off my clothes, walked out back and jumped in the pool stark naked. I was standing in the middle of the pool with my eyes closed and my head back so that my ears were underwater when Dina got home. She saw what I was doing and quickly joined me in a similar state of undress.

"I've got to tell you that being welcomed home by a naked man in the swimming pool is not a bad thing," she said. "Feel free to do it every day."

She was standing in water up to her shoulders, although I could see the rest of her body under the surface.

"How'd it go today?" she asked. "What was Valencia's favor all about?"

"Something I wish I hadn't said 'yes' to," I admitted.

"A lot of favors are like that," she said. "Starts little and turns out big."

While I told her everything that happened, as we always seemed to do we found each other in the middle of the pool, bobbing gently in the water. Dina's legs were soon wrapped around my waist and her hands clasped at the back of my neck. My arms were around her, too, with my fingers laced at the small of her back. Thus entwined, her breasts gently rubbed against my chest and our bodies touched in all kinds of spectacularly strategic places.

When I finished my story, she looked down between us.

"Well, well, what do we have there?" she said.

"Something's come up," I said.

"'I'll say," she said, freeing one hand to reach into the water.

By the time Brewster figured out what we were doing and started fussing about it the way he always did, a train wreck wouldn't have distracted us. Convinced that we were doing irreparable harm to each other, if not committing an act of murder before his very eyes, Brewster dashed from one side of the pool to the other and back again, barking like a maniac. A couple of times I thought he might jump in to try to save us from ourselves, but there came a point when he could have jumped on my head for all I cared.

Once we finished thrashing around, still holding each other we shuffled to the side of the pool to show Brewster that we'd managed to survive the ordeal. As far as he was concerned it was a narrow escape, the latest in a long line. Without his noisy vigilance who knows what might have happened?

Brewster got down on his belly and stretched his head out over the pool so that his nose was almost touching the water. Dina scratched one ear then moved her face close so he could kiss her on the nose. It was his way of making sure that she was all right. Apparently I was not worthy of such attention.

"It's a good thing the neighbors are pretty far away," Dina said.

"That's true in more ways than one," I agreed. "Besides the barking, I'm not sure we could carry on out in the open like this if they were right next door."

"*You* were the one bellowing like a wounded moose, big boy," she said. "I was the soul of decorum, as usual. Anyhow, we'd find a way. We always have."

We walked to the steps and climbed out of the pool. I went into the house, got a couple of towels, plus a white wine for Dina and another beer for me, went back out to the deck, and we dried off.

With my towel around my waist, and Dina's towel wrapped under her arms, we sat on the deck and watched Los Arcos in the distance while the horizon grew slowly darker. A parade of fishing boats churned their way back to the marina, packed with sunburned fishermen and, with any luck, maybe even some fish. Among its other attractions, as John Steinbeck pointed out, the Sea of Cortez is the world's largest fish trap.

"You know, I can't get those two out of my head," I said.

"Lilly and Nicole?"

"No, Penn and Teller," I said. "I mean, it's not every day that I run into a couple of pistol-packing female PIs, one straight, one gay, and both of them living in a trailer in another country far from home. It's a pretty strange combination."

We watched the sunset as the day's heat disappeared fast. As happened most days, a light ocean breeze kicked up with the change of temperature.

"Where are they from?" Dina asked.

I admitted that I didn't know.

"Some detective you are."

"Valencia will find all that out. I was just priming the pump so they'd talk."

"You know, Ethan, it's not really so strange," Dina said.

"What?"

"In my new business I've had to learn about all kinds of tourism," she explained. "Single women who go on the road in an RV or a camper are more and more common these days. Nicole and Lilly aren't that unusual, except that in coming down here they probably ranged a little further a field than most."

"Really?"

Dina turned to see if I was kidding, or if I was really interested.

"Seriously, go on," I said, encouraging her. "I had no idea."

"Sometimes it's a woman alone – usually widows or divorcees – but more often they team up," she said. "A lot of women who traveled in RVs with their husbands and enjoyed it don't want to stop when their husbands die. It's a way of staying connected to the life they had. Another factor is that people are retiring earlier and women are more independent. They've even got organizations. I think one of them is called the Wandering Individuals Network, or WIN. Something like that, anyway. They tend to run into each other on the road and become their own support group. It gives them a sense of community. Some even live on the road full time. It can be cheaper than living in a house or apartment and you can come and go as you please visiting friends, relatives, or whoever. They're not big spenders, not like the mobs of golfers and fishermen who come down here for a blowout. But it's a growing trend and the tourism business is starting to pay attention to it. Whether your two women fit the profile I have no idea, but it's not that unusual."

The sun was going down fast, as it always seemed to here. Only a few thin tendrils of light were scattered over the darkness of the sea. In those places, the water seemed to glow like long veins of gold. In the distance, we could see one of the party boats that go out every day for a sunset cruise, where fifty bucks or so gets you a nice sunset, all the liquor you can drink, and a boat ride. Even at this distance, we could hear the faint thumping of the bass from whatever kind of music played on board.

We laughed at that kind of thing now, but we did it the first time we came to Cabo. It's like visiting Paris and going for a cruise on the Seine in the *Batteau Mouche*. Sure it's hopelessly touristy, but it's still fun.

"Probably the only thing that makes Lilly and Nicole exceptional is that one's gay and the other isn't," Dina said, still chewing on her earlier thought. "Usually you see gays or straights traveling together, the way any couple would. In a way, it's probably convenient. At least they're not competing for men."

"They're work partners, too," I said. "I got the feeling that while they probably compete in lots of ways they look out for each other at the same time. It takes all kinds, I guess."

"'It takes all kinds' - come up with that one all by yourself, did you?" asked Dina.

"Yep," I nodded. "Many wonder how I do it?"

"A better question might be why," she said.

CHAPTER 7

AFTER FINISHING my door-to-door work at *El Campeador* the next day, I was out by the pool reading Michael Palin's entertaining diary about his days with Monty Python when Valencia called.

"We have a ransom note," he said. "Interested?"

"How do you mean?"

"Would you like to see it?"

I could feel myself being sucked in and didn't like the feeling. You could even say that it sucked.

"I appreciate what you did yesterday, especially with the two women." It was as if Valencia sensed my hesitation and intended to overcome it even before it was expressed. "The *senoras* were quite helpful as far as they could be. They're probably excellent investigators at home, although it was very foolish of the one to think about taking a shot."

"Where are they from, by the way?" I asked.

"California," he replied. "Sacramento."

"I assume you confiscated their weapons?" I asked.

"I thought it best," he said. "I promised to return them when they leave, along with a permit that allows them to carry guns. If they're stopped for any reason, they can show it. I also requested that they remain here until further notice. They did not seem to mind. There are worse places to be."

I didn't say anything and silence grew fat between us. Sometimes silence is a good thing and I don't mind it, but not this time. Valencia had me hooked and he knew it. While I was curious and wanted to take a look at the ransom note, I had a strange feeling that once I did I would be crossing a line of some kind and couldn't go back even if I wanted to.

Oh, to hell with it, I thought. It wasn't as if I was taking a blood vow.

"Yeah, I'd like to see the note," I admitted.

"I will be in my office for the rest of the afternoon," he said. "Come anytime."

The Cabo San Lucas police station is a modest one-story white-washed cinder-block building on a badly paved side street downtown. Although it's only a couple of years old, it's the typical bleak and charmless cop shop that can be found anywhere in the world. It even has the same smell, a combination of anxiety, testosterone, copy machines going full blast, and cheap cleansers fighting a losing battle.

I checked in at the desk. A ridiculously young cop in an oversized uniform that was so heavily starched it didn't seem to bend when he walked led me to Valencia's office. The office was small, maybe twelve-by-twelve, with a window on the wall behind the desk that looked out at the dirt parking lot in back of the building. There was a file cabinet in one corner and two cheap visitors' chairs facing the desk, which was gray metal like the file cabinet. The desk was clear except for an institutional green telephone, a black Mont Blanc pen, and a yellow legal pad. Valencia was an orderly man. Although the heat had broken and there was a light breeze coming in from the ocean, a wall air conditioner chattered with furious efficiency. If the room was any colder I wouldn't have been surprised to see a penguin waddle by.

I sat in one of the visitors' chairs. The joints creaked as they took my two hundred pounds.

"It's like Ice Station Zebra in here," I grumped.

"I like it cool," Valencia shrugged. "It keeps me alert."

He rose out of his chair and went to a Mr. Coffee that was on top of the filing cabinet. He poured coffee into a white mug for himself, added two packs of sweetener, some kind of cream substitute, and motioned with the pot to ask if I wanted some.

Although it was tempting to have something hot in this ice cube of an office, I shook my head. Valencia returned to his desk and opened a drawer. He pulled out a red file folder and carefully withdrew a sheet of paper from the folder.

"Here is the note."

Using his index finger, he pushed the sheet of paper across his desk.

"It arrived with the morning mail."

It was a copy, cleanly typed, no doubt by a printer, on a standard sheet of white eight-and-a-half-by-eleven paper. There was no salutation. It said what it had to say and nothing more.

While it was coming along pretty well, my Spanish was still clumsy. I could read it okay, although not with great speed, and speak it in a kind of goofy Spanglish way that was endlessly amusing to the locals, but I still had a hard time following the spoken word. Fortunately, since this was a note, I didn't have to.

"Es tiempo que Jorge Tolsa pagado el daño que él ha hecho a nuestro México hermoso. Con su cogida comparte el tiempo el ha hecho millones que contaminaba paraíso en el nombre del beneficio, arruinando a las playas, a los océanos, al mismo aire

que respiramos, e incluso a sus empleados, que trabajan las largases horas para los salarios de hambre así que el Tolsa codicioso puede llenar encima de sus Pesos."

"Habríamos preferido ir después de este enemigo de nuestro país por los canales pacíficos y legales, pero el gobierno está en su bolsillo. Lamentamos estos métodos violentos, pero no hay otra opción a ayudar a proteger el mayor bueno y financiar nuestro movimiento a la subsistencia México que es el país hermoso ha estado siempre."

"Maria Tolsa es ilesa, hasta ahora. Si el cerdo Tolsa la desea detrás él pagará cientos veinte millones de Pesos. Si no, él la verá después en pedazos. Tolsa será entrado en contacto con con direcciones."

"Una vez más lamentamos estos métodos, pero puede ser que luchemos la influencia de millones con millones."

"Los amigos de Mexico"

Valencia patiently sipped his coffee and stared out the window at his wonderful view of the parking lot while I labored through the translation. I didn't ask for help and he didn't offer any. As best I could tell, it came out like this:

"It is time that Jorge Tolsa paid for the damage he has done to our beautiful Mexico. With his fucking timeshares, he has made millions polluting paradise in the name of profit, ruining beaches, oceans, the very air we breathe, and even his employees, who work long hours for starvation wages so the greedy Tolsa can pile up his pesos."

"We would have preferred to go after this enemy of our country by peaceful and legal channels, but the government is in his pocket. We regret these violent methods, but there is no other choice to help protect the greater good and to finance our movement to keep Mexico the beautiful country is has always been."

"Maria Tolsa is unharmed, so far. If the swine Tolsa wants her back he will pay one hundred and twenty million pesos. If

not, he will next see her in pieces. Tolsa will be contacted with instructions."

"Again, we regret these methods, but we must fight the influence of millions with millions."

"The Friends of Mexico"

I probably didn't have it exactly right, but I was sure that I got the gist. The note was about as subtle as a thumb in the eye. There weren't any nuances to miss.

I pushed the note back across the desk to Valencia.

"A hundred and twenty million pesos is what, about ten million dollars?" I asked.

"Depending on currency fluctuations, you're right, it's in the area of ten million," Valencia said.

"You said you got it in the mail. Where was it mailed from?"

"Here," he replied. "Our mail being what it is the note might have been mailed *before* the kidnapping, although I doubt it."

"Who or what are the Friends of Mexico?" I asked. "Ever hear of them?"

"So far I can't find *anyone* who has heard of them," Valencia admitted. "Not here. Not in Mexico City. Not in the United States. Not in Central or South America. No where at all. It's as if it did not exist until this note."

"It sounds like it might be one of those radical environmental groups that are willing to kill the people who live on the planet in order to save it," I said.

"Judging from the contents of the note, that would seem to be the case," he agreed. "It's either a new group, or an old one with a new name. Perhaps it's a splinter group, or something set up just for the purpose of this kidnapping. That's assuming it's not made up so that we waste our time looking for something that doesn't exist."

"Pretty ambitious, too, if it's real," I said. "Unless my

translation is way off, this doesn't read like it was written to Tolsa. Did it go to somebody else?"

"He received the original," Valencia explained. "Copies went to us and to the newspaper."

"Maybe Tolsa is incidental," I said. "Maybe they mostly want to get the word out to help the cause. A bully pulpit and all that."

"Tolsa may be incidental, but that much money certainly is not," Valencia said. "And I doubt very much that his wife feels incidental just now."

"Good point," I agreed. "By the way, I didn't see anything about the kidnapping in the newspaper or on the internet his morning."

"No, you didn't. And you won't, at least not for the time being. We have an arrangement with the media, the arrangement being that we told them not to publish anything about the kidnapping, here or anywhere else. There will be nothing in print, on television, or on the internet."

Maybe I should have been surprised, but I wasn't. Valencia couldn't get away with that kind of high-handed move in the United States, but this wasn't the United States. Things were different here. That was true not only in the obvious ways, but in ways that were not immediately visible, too. I forgot that sometimes. It was a good thing to keep in mind.

"How long will that kind of embargo hold up?" I asked.

"That is hard to say. The story will get out eventually, but not for a while. I'd say several days perhaps. Until then we bought some time to do our work out of the glare of the spotlight."

I reached over the desk, pulled the note toward me, and read it again.

"They seem especially offended by the timeshares,

don't they?" I said. "This may be a stupid question because I know he's a rich man, but does Tolsa have that much cash?"

Valencia took a sip of his coffee. To someone who didn't know him, he would have seemed calm enough, a young man with a glistening career all laid out before him, assuming that he didn't make any glaring mistakes or step on too many important toes. A stranger probably wouldn't have noticed the eyes that were red from lack of sleep and the tension that stiffened his posture and turned his handsome face into an expressionless mask. He was laboring under a terrible strain with no relief in sight. He hid it well, but he couldn't hide it all. No one could.

I knew the drill. It's pretty much the same everywhere. Valencia was fighting a battle on two fronts. One was the investigation into the kidnapping. That was his job and he was good at it. The other one was bureaucratic, and in some ways it was worse. He wanted to keep his department as the lead agency on the case at the same time a bunch of state and federal agencies probably were trying to big foot their way in. It's been my experience that the more jurisdictions get involved the harder it is to solve a case because the investigation gets in its own way. Instead of sharing information, the competing agencies keep it to themselves because they're competitive and want to ace out the other guys. Back home, the CIA, FBI, NSA, Homeland Security, and who knows how many other agencies all claim to have national security as their goal, but that doesn't keep them from competing with each other, often to the detriment of what they're supposed to do. And that's not even counting the state, county and local cops.

If things went to hell, if, say, Maria Tolsa was butchered and her body sent to her husband in small pieces, well, Jorge Tolsa was a powerful and influential man, the kidnapping and murder would be international news, and somebody would have to take the fall. That somebody would almost certainly be Valencia. If it all worked out, if the kidnappers were caught and Maria Tolsa returned unharmed, the line to take credit for success would stretch from here to Guatemala. If it didn't work out, Valencia would stand alone. It probably was the same all over the world, ugly in many languages.

In the past, Valencia's father could have helped. He was a powerful and mysterious general named Urrea I met not long after we moved to Cabo San Lucas. Along with Valencia, I'd gotten into some trouble on a case I shouldn't have taken in the first place. Valencia was the general's illegitimate son and Urrea helped save our bacon from the federals that were not pleased at our independent behavior and poised to do unpleasant things.

But there was one little problem. The old boy was murdered six months ago, gunned down as he was leaving a Mexico City restaurant by three men using semi-automatic weapons. As far as I knew, no arrests had been made. For one thing, there were too many suspects. The General's past was a little murky. He wasn't always one of the good guys. There were rumors that Valencia enacted his own vengeance on his father's killers, but he never said anything about it and I didn't ask.

"If the Friends of Mexico is what it claims to be, then the two are linked," Valencia said.

My train of thought had clattered off the rails.

"Come again? The two of what linked?" I asked.

Valencia smiled. "You may have noticed that Los Cabos has a lot of timeshares."

I had to laugh. "My friend, you are a master of understatement."

There were times when Los Cabos seemed like wall to

wall timeshares. It was virtually impossible to escape getting pitched to buy one. If a tourist rented a car at the airport, the person behind the car rental desk offered a sweet deal on the car in exchange for attending a tour of some new timeshare project, which was followed by a chance to buy in at some so-called "special" rate, although you didn't have to be Warren Buffet to figure out that all the rates were special all the time. People who worked in restaurants by night sold timeshares by day. Fishing boat captains sold timeshares when they weren't out on the water, and sometimes *when* they were out on the water. All of the major hotels were associated with timeshares in one way or another, too. Check into a hotel and you got pitched. Walk down the street and you got pitched. Go to a restaurant and you got pitched. Buy a souvenir and you got pitched. Timeshares were in the air. Timeshares were everywhere.

The business of selling them attracted an eclectic group of people. A lawyer Dina and I knew years ago in San Francisco retired early so that he and his wife could sail around the world, stopping where and when they felt like it, except that they only got as far as Cabo San Lucas. They put in and decided to stay a while. Why not? They weren't on a schedule. She even took a job as the accounting manager at the marina. After a couple of months, he wanted to do something, too, but didn't want to be consumed by work the way he was back home. He wound up working half days selling timeshares. Two years later, they were still here. He'd become a timeshare gypsy. When one project sold out, he moved on the next one, and there was always a next one. He was pretty good at it, too, although I tried not to hold it against him.

"Tolsa has many timeshare projects either finished, under construction, or in the planning stage," Valencia continued. "And there will be more after that. He is easily the leader in the field here, with probably more than everyone else combined. Although the government is supposed to regulate how many timeshares can be built in Los Cabos, with his connections there are many who believe that Tolsa is overbuilding. Even if he isn't, his critics say that he has turned his projects, especially the more recent ones, into concrete canyons that will ruin those things that brought people to Los Cabos in the first place."

"He must be making money at it or he wouldn't keep doing it," I said. "That means people are buying, which means they're not offended. Besides, they say that or something like it almost every time somebody builds something anywhere in the world. Sometimes it's true, but sometimes it isn't. A lot of the griping might just be sour grapes, too. Like you said, Tolsa's the top dog. Maybe it's just a bunch of envious competitors yapping at his heels?"

Valencia got up to refill his coffee. This time I accepted his offer for a cup of my own. I felt like I was on the verge of frostbite. Maybe I could dip my fingers in it?

"How much coffee is that today?" I asked.

"Too much," he admitted.

He took a sip, made a face, put the cup on his desk, and pushed it aside.

"Are you familiar with how profitable the timeshare business can be?" he asked.

"I've never paid much attention to the details," I admitted. "I never had reason to. Despite their reputation, I know that a lot of people like them. You're buying recreation, a lifestyle, and dependability, among other things. They're lousy investments, too. Re-sales are such a small fraction of the original price they're practically given away. A lot of the time people cave into the pitch, buy on impulse, and regret it later. They're certainly not for everyone."

I thought about it for a moment.

"I guess most of what I know is from the buyer's point of view. I take it from what you said that the business is pretty profitable, which doesn't surprise me."

"You might put it that way," he explained. "The truth is that it is practically a license to steal."

Valencia pulled his yellow legal pad close and began writing.

"Let's say you have a timeshare development of two hundred units," he said. "Some developments are smaller and some are larger; most are larger, especially the newer ones. Typically, timeshares are sold by the week; say fifty weeks a year per unit, with two weeks off for maintenance of the facility."

I did the math in my head.

"So your two hundred unit timeshare development sells ten thousand weeks, right?"

Valencia smiled. "Very good. You didn't even need a calculator."

I was surprised to find that I was pleased at the compliment. I felt like a grade-school student who just got a gold star, even if I was too old to wear it on my forehead.

"Most developments are a mix of studio, one bedroom and two bedroom units," he continued. "A studio is least expensive; the two bedroom unit is most expensive."

I rolled my eyes.

"Thank you, professor. I'm ready for the pop quiz now."

He ignored me and plowed on.

"Let's say the average price is eighteen thousand dollars per week per unit. What does that come to?"

"Sorry, but this time I *will* need a calculator," I admitted.

Valencia took a solar-powered calculator out of the middle drawer of his desk and began punching buttons.

"Eighteen thousand times fifty is nine hundred thousand," he said. "That's just for one unit for a year. We were talking about a two hundred unit complex, so it would be nine hundred thousand times two hundred, or one hundred eighty million dollars from one complex."

"But that's not all profit," I said. "It costs money to build, hire staff, do the maintenance, bribe inspectors, whatever."

For a nano-second, Valencia actually smiled at my little joke.

"But not as much as you probably think," he said. "Each timeshare owner is charged an annual maintenance fee depending on the size of the unit. Let's say the average is six hundred dollars, which is almost certainly low and much more than it actually costs. For our two hundred unit complex, that's six million dollars a year, which pays for the maintenance, the staff, what it takes to run the complex, plus a nice profit. In short, once a project is up and running it not only pays for itself, it makes even more money, which helps the owner build even more."

"What about construction?" I asked.

"That's harder to calculate," he admitted. "But it's not impossible. As you know, labor is cheap in Mexico. What is done by machinery in your country is done by muscle and sweat here. Workers are paid very little and that means construction costs are low, ridiculously so by American standards. Twenty dollars a day buys a hard-working laborer, less than what one of yours is paid per hour. A very attractive two hundred unit timeshare project can be built for fifteen to twenty million dollars, probably closer to fifteen million."

I was surprised at how the numbers played out. I knew timeshares were profitable, but I didn't know they were *that* profitable.

"And remember that Jorge Tolsa has many such projects here and elsewhere," Valencia concluded. "I haven't even included the restaurants, bars and night clubs at these places. They make money, too, a great deal of it. He also has his own fishing fleet that services all his projects, plus his own rental car and excursion companies."

"So the upshot is that you're saying Tolsa can handle the ransom out of petty cash?" I asked.

"It's still a lot of money but yes, I'm sure he can handle it easily," Valencia said. "I'm surprised the kidnappers didn't ask for more than they did. By the way, while they refer to pesos and cash in the note, I'm sure they'll want it in some other form, depending on how sophisticated they are. Perhaps American dollars handled by some kind of transfer to an anonymous account in some far off corner of the world. Bermuda, Andorra, the Cayman Islands, Liechtenstein, Switzerland; who can say? Maybe there will be more than one location. Maybe there will be several. By the time we track the money, if they're smart they will have moved it elsewhere, and then somewhere else after that, with us always a step or two behind."

"So what happens now?"

I knew how it likely would go in the States, but I wasn't sure about Mexico.

Valencia reached for his coffee and started to take a sip. Before the white mug got to his lips he changed his mind and put it back on his desk.

"At some point we will receive another note detailing

the specifics of the ransom, including when and how it will be handled," he said. "As I said, they won't want it all in cash. That much cash is too heavy and bulky, even in large bills. They may even want it in some form that can't be traced the way accounts can, say, middling size diamonds or other gems that are easy to unload anywhere in the world. However it's done, they may ask for a small amount of cash, too, probably American dollars in non-sequential small denominations. Say a hundred thousand, perhaps less, perhaps more. It depends on how much money the kidnappers already have available to them and how many of them there are. At the same time, to increase the sense of urgency and to frighten Jorge Tolsa even more than he already is, the note will make more - and more graphic - threats against Maria Tolsa. In the meantime, of course, our investigation will continue. They might even send a body part, say, a finger. It might belong to Maria Tolsa and it might not."

"Unfortunately, at the moment you don't have much to investigate," I said. "There's the phantom boat, the Friends of Mexico, whatever that is, and the fact that the ransom note was mailed from here, which probably doesn't mean anything, and might even be a red herring. Do I have it about right?"

Valencia nodded.

"We will do everything we can to reassure Tolsa and find his wife, but the reality is that she probably will die and we may recover only a portion of the money if we recover anything," he said. "We might catch some of the kidnappers, perhaps even all of them, but that won't do Maria Tolsa much good, will it?"

CHAPTER 8

I LEFT Valencia's ice box and his depressing conversation with a strong need to work out, to do something that would leave me on the verge of virtuous and well-earned exhaustion. I didn't have any tennis scheduled, but my gear was in my car. I drove over to the club to see if I could pick up a match.

In Cabo, the big sports are fishing and golf, with a dozen world class courses designed by the top names in the business. Unless you fight a big fish for several hours, fishing isn't much of a workout. I never cared much for it anyway. For me, deep sea fishing is a good way to ruin a nice boat ride. As for golf, if I ever blow out a knee on the tennis court I might take it up, but I'd rather not. It takes too long, for one thing. It's easy to blow a whole day on eighteen holes. For another, there are the golfers. Being trapped for five hours on a golf course with a toilet seat manufacturing titan from Lincoln, Nebraska, might make me want to stick my head in an oven. Then there's the sport itself. Someone once described golf as an exercise in Scottish pointlessness designed for people who aren't strong enough to throw telephone polls at each other.

That's pretty much how I feel about it. I'd rather toss tele-phone poles.

La Gaviota was a club with a dozen clay courts, an Olympic-size swimming pool, a decent work-out facility that was never too crowded, a sauna, and a steam room. It also had nothing for me to pick up. Nobody needed a partner for doubles. I didn't see anyone at loose ends and looking for singles either. No residents. No sun-burned and slightly hunger over tourists looking for a match. Nothing.

Then fortune smiled, as fortune sometimes does. One of the club pros had time to kill until he was scheduled for a lesson with a bunch of kids from several of Cabo's upper class families. The pro was a big rangy guy named Clancy who'd played tennis for the University of Arizona. His dream of turning pro was ruined when his knee was crushed in an automobile accident during his sophomore year. The rehab went well enough, but he knew he'd never make it in the big show. Now he was in his late twenties, single, and making a nice living as a club pro in Cabo San Lucas. He agreed to hit with me for an hour until his session with the urchins started. Of course, I'd pay for the privilege, but it was money well spent.

The difference between pros and club players in tennis is the same as it is between pros and amateurs in everything else. People who do it as a sideline don't have a chance against people who do it for a living. Pros do it every day. They've been well taught, they do everything right, and they make it look easy.

Years ago, when we still lived in Southern California, I took Dina to an indoor pistol range. As usual, I shot against the guy who owned the place. We bet a bottle of scotch and I lost. I always did. An endless supply of free liquor was why he never charged me.

It was the first time Dina had come with me. As we walked back to the car, she said, "I thought you were a good shot."

"I *am* a good shot, but he's a pro," I explained. "What you just saw was one of my better days, but I'll never beat a guy who does it every day. It's second nature to him. He doesn't even have to think about it. The firearm is like an extension of his hand."

Over the next hour, Clancy ran me all over the Baja Peninsula. He had the right feel for a club pro. He maintained his easy superiority but still let me play. That's the kind of thing that keeps a customer happy and coming back. At its best, there's a rhythm to tennis that's almost musical when everything works. When that happens, it has a lot to do with the quality and style of the opposition. Thanks to Clancy's help, I had it going today and it felt good.

I was breathing hard and sweating heavily when we finished the hour. I was tired, but it was a satisfying tired, exactly what I wanted.

When we shook hands at the net, Clancy said, "You hit pretty well today."

"Thanks," I said. "I appreciate your diplomacy, not to mention your restraint."

Clancy laughed. "Give me a call. I'll be glad to hit anytime."

He went on to his lesson with the kiddies and I went into the clubhouse. As usual, several of the younger mothers stayed and watched Clancy work with their children. Hmm, I thought. It probably was not a bad thing to be a young good-looking tennis pro in Cabo San Lucas.

Thirty minutes later, freshly showered and combed and glowing with virtue, I threw my tennis bag in the trunk and got in behind the wheel, savoring the usual covetous looks at my cool wheels. I drive a '65 Mustang convertible. It's a fully-restored classic painted Arcadian blue with a white top, white leather interior and a 289 cubic inch engine with a manual transmission. Several years ago, after a case up in Thousand Oaks north of LA, my client offered the car instead of a check. I grabbed it and never looked back. Every time I get behind the wheel I can feel my self-esteem rise to unseemly heights.

I knew that I should do something constructive, but didn't have a clue what that might be. The truth was that the kidnapping had me all churned up and I didn't know why. Sure, I'd helped Valencia a little, but other than that it was none of my business. Bad things happen every day all over the world. So why was I fixated on this one?

After sitting for a while and brooding about it, I decided to drive over to Dina's office. In some ways she knew me better than I knew me. Maybe she'd have an explanation? Sometimes just talking about something helps it unravel.

Dina's office consisted of one room on the third floor, with a million-dollar view of the marina from a big picture window. Not a sound from the outside world could be heard inside the office. It was as if the place was hermitically sealed. The carpet was plush and the office was cool. She figured that in about six months or so she'd have to hire a secretary and move to bigger quarters, but in the meantime she was content with the nimble simplicity of a one-woman operation.

When I walked in, she was on the telephone and waved me to a chair.

"I know it's not as polished as Cancun," she said. "It doesn't have the big city feel of Puerto Vallarta or Acapulco either. But that's part of its appeal. The mix of old and new and rough and smooth is what people like about Cabo. It's not just another cookie-cutter resort. Down market or upscale, you can go either way here and that's a real advantage, not to mention the obvious stuff like some of the best fishing and golf in the world."

She listened for a while, impatiently nodding her head.

"Okay, let me know if you need anything else," she said.

Dina slammed the telephone in its cradle.

"Dumb ass," she said with considerable feeling.

"Well, yes, some days," I said. "But I like to think that's not true all the time."

She laughed, got up, walked around from behind her desk and gave me a smooch.

"Not you, sweetie. It's this travel magazine block-head. He's having a hard time figuring out where Cabo fits into, I quote, "the greater scheme of Mexico tourism," whatever that's supposed to mean. Mostly he's a fatuous twit. I think he's just trying to get a free trip down here."

She smiled. It was like watching the sun come up.

"So what brings you here?" she asked, perching on the arm of my chair.

I looked around the office.

"Do you know that you have more pictures of our dog than you have of me?" I asked. "I counted while you were on the phone."

"Don't push your luck," she said. "Tell me what's going on."

I told her about my problem with the kidnapping, how it was keeping me all roiled up. Valencia hadn't asked for any more of my help, but I was on the verge of volunteering anyway, even though I knew that I shouldn't. There was something going on inside my head and I didn't understand it.

Dina left her perch on my chair, planted herself in the other client chair, and took my hand in both of hers.

"I love you, but you're such a goof sometimes," she said.

"Uh, thanks, I think. I love you, too. "

"You really don't get it?"

"Really."

"It's the family thing," she said. "Nails you every time."

And that's when I saw it. She was right. I should have known from the beginning.

When I was five years old, I watched while my mother and father were beaten to death.

My father had just bought a new car; the first new car he ever owned. With loving hands, he washed and vacuumed it every Saturday morning. For some reason, a couple of hard case addicts decided that they had to have it. They saw it in a grocery store parking lot one afternoon and followed my father home to find out where he lived. It was never clear why they wanted that car. I'm not sure they knew. Except to my father, it wasn't that special.

We were asleep they came into our house through an unlocked sliding door and crept up the stairs. They had baseball bats in their hands and fresh tracks in their arms. I was awakened by strange and angry voices in our house and stumbled down the hall to my parents' bedroom, where I saw two strange men standing over their bed.

I remember feeling scared. Something was wrong, but I didn't know what and the fear was like a lead weight in my chest. I said, "Mom? Dad?" One of the men turned and saw a little boy in cowboy pajamas standing just inside the bedroom door. Without a word, he stepped over and backhanded me so hard that I bounced off the wall. My father come roaring out of the bed, his hands clutching at the man's throat. I saw the other guy swing his bat, I heard my mother scream, and that was the last thing I remembered.

They found me two days later. I was huddled in a ball in a corner of the bedroom, covered with my parents' blood. The two men beat them to death and took the car. My dad never missed a day of work and when he missed two days in a row his boss called. When he didn't get an answer, he drove to our house to see if anything was wrong. When no one answered the door he called the police. The killers were caught within twenty four hours after that, not exactly great criminal minds. They went to prison. For all I know they're still inside. Or maybe they're dead by now? I never bothered to find out. What did it matter?

I still don't remember the rest of what happened that night. I'm not even sure that I remember what little I think I remember. It might just be something my subconscious constructed to fill the void. The trauma started a lifelong pattern of what psychiatrists call disassociation. There have been times when things got tough or something bad was about to happen and I went away inside my head. Not always and not often, but often enough. I'm told that I do it either to protect myself from what's going on around me, or to protect myself from what I'm about to do because I know that what I'm about to do isn't a good thing. When it happens, most of the time even people who know me pretty well don't see anything different about my behavior. I just seem a little vague, as if I'm distracted. When I disassociate I'm not in control of what I'm doing and, on a conscious level, don't even know I'm doing it. It usually doesn't last very long and most of the time it's harmless, but it's never a good thing. One of the dangers of disassociation is that you can go away and never come back. Or you might do something that you never would have done if you'd been in control of yourself. I have nightmares, too, sometimes, intense and ugly nightmares. With off-and-on therapy, it's gotten better over the years, although there have been times when I did things that I regret. All the shrinks I've seen agree that if I could remember the rest of what happened the night my parents were killed it would be a major breakthrough. It probably would, but it hasn't happened. The truth is that while part of me wants to remember, there's another part that wants to keep it buried so deep that I never have to see it again.

So what mental health people call family issues have a way of ringing my bells. The kidnapping of Jorge Tolsa's wife would probably qualify as a family issue.

It's like they say, no matter where you go, you take yourself with you.

I realized that neither one of us had said anything for a while.

"You're right, of course," I admitted. "Why the hell didn't I see it? I wonder what happens now."

"If we're lucky, maybe the answer to that is nothing," Dina said.

CHAPTER 9

It was expensive sheet of bonded paper folded inside an expensive envelope and delivered by a neatly barbered young man dressed in black pants, black loafers, and a short-sleeved white shirt, no doubt all of it expensive. There was something so crisp and efficient about his manner that it made the outfit seem like a uniform.

He handed me the envelope when I answered the door, but only after he confirmed that I was, in fact, *"Senor Cookshrank."*

"Close," I said. "You're very close."

Both the envelope and the paper inside had the word "Tolsa" inscribed in heavy gold script. On the envelope it was where the return address goes. On the paper, it was at the top in the middle. I could feel the weight of it in my hand. Impressive; but then it was supposed to be.

I read the words on the paper. When I finished, I read them again. I knew that I hadn't missed anything the first time, but reading it again gave me something to do while I tried to figure out what the hell was going on. Although the wording was a little awkward, it was written in English so that I didn't have to labor over a translation. It was probably dictated in Spanish, and then translated for my benefit.

"*Sir,*"

"*I request the honor of a meeting at my home this afternoon at four p.m. It is a matter of great importance to me and I beg that you attend.*"

"*If you would be so kind, please inform the messenger of your decision. If you wish, transportation will be provided.*"

"*Most sincerely,*"

"*Jorge Tolsa*"

I looked up from the note to the messenger, who hadn't as much as shifted his weight from one foot to the other.

"Do you know what this is all about?" I asked.

He shook his head. "No, *senor*, I do not," he replied in English that was heavily accented and carefully spoken.

"And do you know it's redundant to say 'this afternoon at four p.m.?'" I asked.

He looked at me as if I'd just beamed in from Neptune. Why say something so idiotic? I was stalling for time, that's why. What did Jorge Tolsa want with me?

The messenger waited. Then he waited some more. I felt the pressure of his presence working on me. Finally I decided to go with it. If Tolsa intended to pique my curiosity he certainly succeeded. Why pretend otherwise? There wasn't any harm in a simple meeting. It was no big deal. Right?

Sure, Cruickshank, whatever you say. I'd learned a long time ago that I could talk myself into anything.

"All right, tell *Senor* Tolsa I'll be there at four," I said. "I'll provide my own transportation."

The messenger made a motion that was somewhere between a nod and a bow and practically backed out the door. The movement was so servile I was tempted to throw him a coin. I watched as he climbed into a big black Lincoln Navigator and drove away. The doors were inscribed with the name "Tolsa." In gold, too.

Like I said, impressive.

CHAPTER 10

I STOPPED at the gate house at the entrance to the Tolsa compound, mostly because the barrier was down and it would have been tacky to barrel on through.

A uniformed guard with a Glock nine holstered on his hip checked my ID while another guard cradling a Kalashnikov in his arms stood to one side where he'd have a clear shot if I tried anything.

After making sure that my face matched the picture on my license, the guard consulted a clipboard that probably listed the names of everyone who was expected today. Satisfied that I was who I claimed to be, after writing down my license number he waved me out of the Mustang and motioned for me to put my hands on the door so he could pat me down. It was a sloppy frisk with a lot more attitude than effectiveness, but I decided not to mention it.

When the guard finished, I got back in the Mustang.

"You will park there, in front of the house," he said, pointing to the big house about seventy five yards down a cobblestone driveway that cut through the manicured lawn like a scar.

I drove to the spot, got out of the Mustang, and walked to the front door. The impression was of a rambling stone villa with bougainvillea and many balconies and intruder lights and fountains and video cameras and graceful statues and walls with razor wire and a putting green and two more guards walking large dogs on short leashes and a lot of palm trees. All the bristling security would have been more impressive if I hadn't known what happened just after midnight a few days ago.

The door was made of some kind of old dark wood. At least it looked like it. I was willing to bet that it was a relatively new door made to look old and probably didn't weigh nearly as much as it seemed.

Before I could knock or press the buzzer, the door slowly opened, as if by itself, like the start of a bad horror movie. I hesitated for a moment and then stepped inside. A little rat-faced man wearing the same uniform of dark trousers and white shirt that the messenger wore this morning stepped from behind the door and gave a nervous little bow.

"Please, *senor*, you are to follow me," he said, scuttling away.

I followed him across the tiled foyer. We passed though an enormous living room with a cathedral ceiling and massive wooden beams that looked like no one had ever lived in it, through another immense room with a pool table in the middle, a full-size bar at one end, and red leather wing chairs along the walls, and into a glass-enclosed sun room that looked out over a swimming pool that was only a little smaller than the Great Salt Lake, complete with a rock waterfall that was at least twelve feet tall.

The room was furnished in more leather, this time a

rich dark brown. Even the coffee table was covered in leather. The décor was so out of place in such a light and sunny room that the contrast was grotesque. What I'd seen of Tolsa's home so far resembled what would happen if someone took a London gentlemen's club, circa 1900, or so, and put it down where it would seem most out of place. What was the name of Sherlock Holmes' brother? Mycroft? The fat one who was always hanging around his club in London? With a brandy snifter in one hand, he would have felt right at home in *Casa Tolsa*. You'd probably find him in one of the wing chairs reading a copy of the London Times.

But instead of Mycroft Holmes, it was Valencia was sitting in one of the chairs. I did not expect to see him here. On the other hand, until this morning I didn't expect to see me here either.

The man sitting on the other side of the leather coffee table from Valencia rose to his feet, except that he didn't get up as much as rather elegantly unfold. Two or three inches taller than my six two, he was dressed in a white short sleeve planter's shirt, white linen pants, and white Guccis with gold buckles and no socks, all of which contrasted beautifully with his lightly toasted skin. His thick silver hair was swept back from his forehead and curling in the back. His face was long with a strong aquiline nose. He looked like royalty, or what royalty ought to look like but never does, and moved with an easy liquid grace. Judging from appearances, I'd guess that he was in his fifties, but if this was who I thought it was then he was at least twenty years older.

He offered his hand. "*Senor* Cruickshank, I am Jorge Tolsa. It is a pleasure."

The handshake was dry, warm and firm, but not too firm, as if he'd graduated *magna cum laude* from handshake school. Hell, Tolsa probably owned the handshake school.

"Please, sit down."

He motioned to a leather couch that faced the coffee table so that Tolsa was on one side, Valencia on the other, and my back was to the Great Salt Lake.

When I sank into the cushions they made a pleasurable hiss. I had the urge to make the same kind of sound. The leather was so indescribably soft and buttery that touching it was practically a sensual experience.

"Would you like some refreshment?" Tolsa asked.

"No thank you."

"And you, Captain?" he asked Valencia. "Would you like more coffee?"

"*Gracias,* but no," Valencia replied.

It was the kind of offer that any host would have made, but coming from Tolsa there was a kind of anachronistic courtliness about it. He returned to his chair, hiked one leg over the other and flicked something invisible off the perfect crease in his trousers. Linen wrinkles easily, at least it does when I wear it, but you wouldn't know it by looking at Jorge Tolsa. There wasn't a wrinkle on him. Not a molecule was out of place. It wouldn't have dared.

"I am grateful that you could come on such short notice, especially since you don't yet know why I asked you here," he said. "Of course, you already know Captain Valencia."

"Yes, I do," I said. "I must say, sir, your home is most impressive."

Tolsa's excessive politeness was catching. With its bristling security, out-of-place furnishings, and daffy contrasts, Tolsa's home was hideous, but I felt obligated to offer a compliment, no matter how weak. "Impressive" was the most neutral word I could think of.

Tolsa acknowledged the *faux* compliment with an almost imperceptible nod.

"I am in the process of updating the security, which will remove some of the more unsightly elements, such as the wire," he explained. "I fear that dogs are a defense of the past, too, although I have grown fond of them. Dogs are noisy and unpredictable. They often attack the wrong people and they are easily distracted. Motion sensors, lasers, and various strategically placed alarms will be much more effective."

All things considered, it was as fine an example of shutting the barn door after the horse was stolen as I'd seen in a long time.

Echoing my thoughts, Tolsa sadly added, "I know what you are thinking; it should have been done long ago. Nothing happened for so many years that I made the mistake of taking our security for granted. I was a fool, an old fool."

There wasn't anything I could say to that so I didn't respond. Valencia apparently agreed with me because he didn't say anything either.

"Now to the business at hand," Tolsa said briskly. "I understand that you have been of great help in Captain Valencia's investigation of my wife's kidnapping. I want you to know that I appreciate it with all my heart. If ever I can help you in any way …."

This time it was my turn to nod in acknowledgement.

"I don't know how much help I've been, but I hope your wife will be returned to you safe and sound," I said. "Have there been any further developments?"

Both Valencia and Tolsa shook their heads.

"The captain and I were discussing it when you arrived," Tolsa said. "It seems to me that we should have learned the specifics about the exchange by now, don't you think?"

"Not necessarily," I said with a quick glance at Valencia to make sure I wasn't stomping all over on his turf.

"By making you wait, the kidnappers show that they are in control," Valencia explained. "The more anxious you are, the more eagerly you'll accede to their demands. At least, that is their assumption."

Tolsa digested that for a moment.

"It's not so different from business, I suppose," he said. "Making the opposition wait makes them eager and even a little annoyed, perhaps too eager and too annoyed, so that soon you have them in your hand ready to be squeezed."

"Something like that," I said. "It could drag out for a long time, or it could end tomorrow."

"At any rate, to the point of our meeting," Tolsa said, bringing an abrupt end to that line of conversation. For all his manners, this was a man used to being in control. "I would like to engage you and Captain Valencia to find my wife. If you accept my offer, I have some information that I believe might be helpful."

I shot another look at Valencia, who was wearing his best poker face.

"But the captain is already investigating," I said. "You couldn't be in better hands. I doubt that there's anything more I could do to help. The case certainly doesn't lack for manpower. Half the law enforcement in Mexico must be looking for your wife."

Tolsa glanced at Valencia, as if to get permission, before he spoke again.

"Alas, I fear that our good Captain is no longer on the case, at least not officially," Tolsa explained. He gestured toward Valencia. "Perhaps you should be the one to explain."

Valencia took a deep breath and let it out slowly, as if he was reluctant to talk about it.

"It's true," he admitted. "My department is no longer involved in the investigation."

"Good God! Why?"

"It was - is - a remarkable mess," he said, continuing as if he hadn't heard me. "There were too many agencies involved, all of them working at cross purposes with each other. It wasn't an investigation as much as a competition for attention. And then ...."

"I can imagine," I interrupted. "It's no different in the United States. It's probably true everywhere. A lot of good people work in law enforcement, but so do a lot of dumb ones. As a bureaucracy gets bigger and bigger, it seems like the dumber you are the higher you rise. When a big multi-jurisdictional case packing a lot of potential publicity like this one comes along everybody gets caught up in the competition to the point where nobody cooperates with anybody else. If they do, it's only in the most superficial way, the bare minimum for what's laughingly called 'interagency cooperation.' With everybody pushing and shoving to get out front, knowledge is power, even when there isn't a hell of a lot to know, so they're obsessed with secrecy. Over time they get conditioned not to tell anybody anything to keep the other guy from stealing the credit, the headlines, and the TV time. At home, or, rather, back in the states, maybe it'd be the FBI fighting with the Treasury guys, and the U.S. Marshal's office fighting with the state cops, who'd be quarrelling with the local and county cops, not to mention umpteen other federal, state and local agencies thrashing around and practically destroying the investigation in their competition with each other. But even if all that's true, I still don't understand why you got yanked off the case."

"You describe it well," Valencia said. "Unfortunately there came a point when I lost my temper."

The poker face disappeared and was replaced with a smile that was almost, but not quite, rueful. Whatever Valencia was sorry about, he wasn't all *that* sorry.

"Actually there were several such points, each one worse than the last, until finally I said things I shouldn't have said to people I shouldn't have said them to," he explained. "In retaliation, my department was taken off the case."

I was sorry to hear that. Valencia was a good cop, one of the best I'd ever seen. It wasn't just something he did; it was what he was. It probably was exactly that commitment that made him blow up. I was knew the feeling, if not the commitment.

"From your comments, you seem to be familiar with such situations, *Senor* Cruickshank." The way Tolsa pronounced it - like *Crookshank* - was exactly right. Like Tolsa's messenger, most Mexicans struggled with my name and usually lost. "I understand that you had some experience with a kidnapping not long before you left the United States."

"Yes I did, but it didn't turn out well," I said. "Not at all."

And wasn't that the understatement of the decade. The police found the baby's body just a few minutes before I was supposed to deliver the ransom at a deserted bench on an Oxnard beach in the middle of the night. When they called to tell me that the baby was dead, I lost it and wound up killing the kidnapper along with a homeless Vietnam veteran who had the bad luck to be hit by one of the shots I fired. I woke up in the mental hospital a couple of weeks later with no memory of what happened. Luckily, I wasn't charged with anything, but the fiasco was the catalyst that led to our move to Mexico. It wasn't the only reason, but it got us motivated.

I didn't mention any of that. There was no point. Instead I waited for Tolsa to take the lead.

"But you do have experience, and that is why I want the two of you to find my wife," he said.

Valencia didn't seem surprised by the offer. He and Tolsa probably went over all this before I got here.

"Despite my earlier grumpy comments about these kinds of cases, there are a lot of good people looking for your wife," I said. "What do you think can the two of us can do that they can't?"

"You can save her," Tolsa replied. "I know how it works as well as you do, at least some of it. The investigation will be – is – widespread. Whether by accident or by good police work, sooner or later something will turn up. At that point, law enforcement at its many levels will move in with all of its technology, its armaments, its helicopters, and its men. When that happens, it will have all the subtlety of an invasion. But there is much corruption in Mexico and this invasion will be too big to be kept secret from the kidnappers. The result will be chaos. My wife will almost certainly be killed or harmed, if not by the kidnappers then by accident by the very people who are trying to save her."

As he talked, tears began coursing down Tolsa's face, although he didn't seem to know it.

"Please understand something, both of you," he said. "I do not care if the kidnappers are caught or go free. I do not care if they go on to kidnap a thousand other people. Perhaps that makes me a terrible man, but so be it. That is the way I feel. All I care about is my wife and getting her back."

"Then why not just pay the ransom as soon as you get the instructions?" I asked.

I was mistaken. Tolsa was aware of his weeping. He reached into his hip pocket, pulled out a handkerchief and carefully patted his cheeks dry. He didn't seem at all embarrassed by his tears. I couldn't think of a reason why he should.

"May I answer?" asked Valencia.

Tolsa nodded. "Of course."

"To our unending shame, it is estimated that some seventy five percent of all the world's kidnappings take place in Mexico, Central, and South America," Valencia explained. "At best, the odds are only fifty-fifty that the person kidnapped will be returned unharmed. In high profile cases such as this one, the odds are much worse than that. Paying the ransom guarantees nothing. It can even make it worse. A dead hostage reveals nothing. The longer it drags out, the higher the odds against success."

I already knew most of that, but I still thought that what might be gained by paying the ransom was better than what we had, which was nothing. Valencia sounded so academic that I had to remind myself we were talking about Tolsa's wife, a woman whose name no one had so far said out loud, as if doing so would put a curse on her.

"So, as you can see, I am a desperate man, *Senor* Cruickshank." Tolsa's tears were gone but he still clutched the wet handkerchief in one hand. "I will do anything, *anything*, to get her back, including pay you very well. Money is no object. I have a great deal of money, but I have only one wife." He paused. "I recall that the two of you worked together before, and quite successfully."

Last year I'd joined up with Valencia and a couple of friends I recruited from Southern California to grab a serial date rapist who drugged and raped 11 women up in Santa Barbara. He'd jumped bail and was hiding out in Cabo. We didn't skirt Mexican law as much as blow it to hell. That was that case when Valencia's father the general saved our skin. At my request, my name was kept out of it, but I wasn't surprised that Tolsa knew. He probably had more sources than the New York Times.

"That was different," I said. "A lot different. In a way, *we* were the kidnappers."

"But perhaps not as different as you think," Tolsa said. "Now, just as then, one bold swift stroke from a small team of men can do the job."

My first reaction was that Tolsa had seen too many movies. Then, when he told us what he was willing to pay to get his wife back, I was sure of it.

"I'm not saying 'yes' yet, so please don't jump to any conclusions, but you mentioned something about having information," I said.

"Yes," Tolsa replied. "I may know who kidnapped Maria."

"I guess that *would* be useful." When nobody else said anything, I kept going. "Okay, I'll bite. Who do you think it was?"

"His name is Bernardo O'Reilly," Tolsa replied. "He once worked for me and became obsessed with my wife. Of course, I didn't know it at the time. It wasn't until much later that I learned about it."

If Tolsa was uncomfortable talking about another man's obsession with his wife he didn't show it. His earlier distress had disappeared and he seemed at ease again, fully able to look at the situation as if he wasn't involved. That kind of cool objectivity was a trait I admired when I saw it in others because I was never any good at it.

"Bernardo O'Reilly?" I asked. "That's an unusual name."

"His father was Irish trash and his mother a Mexican

of the lower classes," Tolsa replied. "He is a mongrel without foundation, standards, or morals."

"How did you find out about this so-called obsession?" I asked.

"There was nothing 'so-called' about it," Tolsa answered. "I saw him openly staring at Maria many times but didn't say anything. I must confess that it didn't particularly bother me. My wife is a beautiful woman. I cannot confront every man who stares at her with lust in his eyes. In a way, I suppose I was even proud of it. But one night I was informed that he was seen peering into the window of her bedroom. I fired him the next day. He threatened me, but the threat was without meaning. What was a man like him going to do to me? Later, several of the staff told me about times they saw him sneaking around Maria's bedroom and how he always seemed to be lurking when she was in the swimming pool or sunbathing, but they were afraid of him and didn't tell anyone.

"How did your wife react when she found out?" asked Valencia.

Apparently this was new information for him, too. When Valencia and Tolsa talked earlier, apparently they didn't get this far.

"She was badly shaken, of course, as anyone would be," Tolsa explained. "How many nights did this man spend at her window? How long had he spied on her? What had he seen? In this terrible era of internet pornography, how badly was her privacy violated? She was terrified and disgusted, of course, as anyone would be."

As Tolsa told the story, a light went off in the dank subterranean recesses of my head.

"Sir, excuse me, but how old is your wife?" I asked.

"She is twenty eight," he said. "We celebrated her birthday just two weeks ago."

I did my best to look like it was just another bit of data to be filed away in the massive Cruickshank gray matter, except that the old gray matter ain't what it used to be. Until a few moments ago I assumed that Maria Tolsa was more or less her husband's age, not some fifty years younger. That changed everything. The money was still the money, especially when it's more than ten million dollars, but now that I knew Maria Tolsa was young and good looking, sexual obsession couldn't be counted out either. In fact, assuming Tolsa was right, sexual obsession was probably a big part of it. I hadn't bothered to ask Valencia about the woman's age, although he obviously knew and all I had to do was ask. It was another reminder; never assume, Cruickshank, never assume. In my defense, until now the woman's age wasn't important to me. Among other things, it probably reduced the chances of getting her back alive, although I wouldn't mention that to Tolsa. It's awfully easy for obsession to turn deadly, especially when it's under the pressure of pursuit.

"When did this happen?" Valencia asked. "When did this O'Reilly work here, for how long, and when did you fire him?"

"He worked for me for not quite one year and I got rid of him about eighteen months ago," Tolsa replied. "I can get the exact dates of his employment if they are important."

"The name is new to me. He didn't come up when we checked the employees," Valencia said, speaking to me. "We looked at everyone who worked here, but only in the past year."

"Maybe it doesn't mean anything anyway?" I said, turning to Tolsa. "If I may be blunt, lusting after your wife and getting fired for it doesn't make this guy a kidnapper."

Valencia asked, "Why didn't you tell us, or someone, before now?"

For the first time, Tolsa's self-assured calm showed a crack. Even when he was weeping, he was never hesitant. But now he didn't seem as sure of himself.

"When I was called in Mexico City and told about what happened … about the kidnapping, it was as if I could not think at all," he explained. "All I felt was paralyzing fear for Maria. Then, when the thoughts of O'Reilly came to me, I realized that if I told the police it would be as I said to you earlier. Maria might not survive the attempt to rescue her. You know that and I know that, although the police would never admit it. But I truly believe that a few men working quietly and quickly could take her from O'Reilly the way I am sure he took her from me. You are those men. You *must* be those men. There is no one else I can turn to. Yes, I could find others, but it would take time, too much time."

Tolsa waved his hands in a kind of inarticulate helplessness. There was a heart-rending sadness to the gesture. For all of his power, aristocratic bearing, and vast fortune, at this moment he was just a desperate old man who'd do anything to get his wife back.

"*Senor* Tolsa, are you willing to tell the appropriate people not to interfere while you supposedly negotiate with the kidnappers and give us time to do our work?" Valencia asked. "You would be lying to them, of course, and there might be repercussions later, but that would give us a chance to do what we need to do without interference."

That one surprised me. Telling law enforcement to butt out while Tolsa did his own thing seemed a little out there, even for Mexico. I wasn't crazy about Valencia talking about "us" either.

Before Tolsa could answer, I interrupted.

"Before this goes any further, you're going to have to explain something to me," I said.

"It is not as strange as it seems," Valencia said, anticipating my question. "It is almost standard procedure in Mexico City, where there were more a hundred kidnappings last year alone. It is less common elsewhere, but certainly not unheard of. Working through private channels can be fast and effective and much less cumbersome."

I had a few questions of my own while I digested all this.

"Forgive me if I seem to be prying, *Senor* Tolsa, but it's necessary if I'm even going to consider taking this on," I said. "In residences like this, the bedrooms are almost always upstairs. But I assume O'Reilly wasn't standing on a ladder when he was seen looking into your wife's bedroom window. That would have been a little obvious. From what I saw when I came in, the upper rooms all have balconies anyway, which would make it harder to see anything. Why is her bedroom on the ground floor? That also made it a lot easier for the kidnappers."

"Your question is perfectly reasonable," Tolsa replied. "Many years ago, when she was just a child, Maria was caught on the fourth floor of a building during an earthquake. The building collapsed and she was trapped in the rubble for several hours, although she was not harmed other than cuts and bruises. The experience left her with a terrible fear of sleeping higher than the first floor. She does not mind flying. That's different. She has no fear of heights. Her greatest fear is being trapped inside a collapsed building. When she travels, she arranges to stay on the ground floor whenever possible so she can more easily escape if anything happens."

Fair enough, I thought.

"If it was O'Reilly who kidnapped your wife - and

keep in mind there is no proof of that despite your suspi-
cions - do you have any information about his
background?"

"Not really," Tolsa admitted. "I have too many
employees to take the time to learn about the background
of every one. Perhaps someone who works for me might
have something. I do have the impression that he has
certain radical beliefs and perhaps surrounds himself
with friends who believe the same nonsense. Such people
often do."

"Do you have *anything* on this guy?" I asked. "Did he
fill out forms when he went to work for you? An applica-
tion? Something for taxes? Anything like that?"

Tolsa shook his head. "Many, perhaps even most, of
my employees are paid in cash. They prefer it and,
frankly, it is less expensive for me. Also, except for a few
key people who have been with me for years they tend to
come and go with frequency. Unfortunately this O'Reilly
was one of them. As far as I know, except for his dates of
employment we have no record of him at all."

I looked at Valencia. "Are you okay with all this?"

"It's worth pursuing," he replied. "I'm going ahead
with it no matter whether you say yes, or no."

I told Tolsa that I needed to speak with Valencia in
private. He suggested that we step out back by the Great
Salt Lake.

"All right, tell me why you're doing this?" I had to
practically shout to be heard over the roar of the waterfall. "If Tolsa's right - and that's a big 'if' - with good luck
maybe we can pull this thing off, but I have the feeling
there'll be a lot of really outstanding opportunities for
bad luck along the way. And we don't even know what it
is we'd be pulling off yet."

Valencia's face was expressionless, but his eyes were
hard as marbles.

"I did not care for their attitude," he said.

"Whose attitude?" Then it came to me. "You mean the big shots who yanked you off the case?"

"Yes."

"And you want to find this woman, solve the case, and shove it up their backside like a broomstick?"

Valencia smiled, but there was no mirth in it.

"Your elegant words capture my feeling exactly."

As motivation goes, that wasn't bad. A lot of people say that revenge isn't worth it, but I've never been one of them. There are times when nothing but revenge will do.

We went back inside and I told Tolsa that I'd join Valencia to try to find his wife, which led to grateful handshakes all around.

Without having anything specific in mind, I added, "You should understand that this could easily wind up being more than two men can handle. In fact, it probably will. If that happens we'll need help, or maybe some kind of equipment or support I can't think of right now. If we do, will you back us up?"

"You will have whatever you need whenever you need it," Tolsa promised. "Just call me; money, material, equipment, men, anything at all. If there is no time, get what you need and I will reimburse you. In the meantime, I think it best that we tell no one on my staff because the fewer people who know about you the better it is. You will deal directly with me and only me. Your decisions are my decisions."

There didn't seem to be anything more to say. Valencia and I agreed to meet for breakfast in the morning. In the meantime, we'd both check around to see if we could find anything on Bernardo O'Reilly. Neither one of us voiced the thought, but I knew that we both wondered if Tolsa's suspicion was any good. Or was it just the desire of a desperate man to do something, anything, in a situation where he had no control? Sure, O'Reilly prob-ably ogled the hell out of Maria Tolsa, but that didn't mean that he recruited a gang, kidnapped her, and killed four men doing it.

As I walked out to the Mustang, I muttered, "Dina will not be thrilled about this."

Valencia didn't respond. I wasn't even sure that he heard me.

CHAPTER 11

DINA'S MERCEDES convertible was parked in front of the house when I got home. She hadn't bothered to put the top up. Unless it was raining, or threatening rain, she rarely did.

She was in back by the pool having a glass of iced tea and going through the mail. We got much less junk mail in Mexico than we did in the states, which was one good reason to leave the country right there. Brewster was lying happily at her side and greeted me with a mighty thumping of his tail. There was nothing he liked better than having his people at home where they could pay attention to him.

"Hey, sweetums," she said, tilting her head so I could give her a smooch.

"Hiya, kid." I pointed at her glass. "Need a refill?"

She shook her head. "Not yet."

"How about a walk?" I asked. "We can take the boy down to the beach and let him run."

"Sure," she said, putting her tea down and rising out of the chair.

We kicked off our shoes and walked down the winding path to the beach, with Brewster frolicking madly along the way, taking ten steps to our one. He loved the beach. He'd run until he was exhausted and barely had enough strength left to stagger back up to the house, where he'd drink about fourteen gallons of water, most of it out of the toilet.

In the United States, in most places letting our dog run on the beach was illegal. In Mexico, nobody cared. I liked that.

It had rained overnight and the sky had that stunning quality that makes everything look closer and clearer. The lines of the houses above the beach were sharper and more detailed and the colors were brighter and cleaner. A red towel someone left on the white sand looked like a splendid flower. The usual late-afternoon breeze had kicked up and the bright blue of the ocean was flecked with a dozen or more white sails, craft that went out to get in a couple of hours sailing before sundown. When we moved to Cabo, we intended to take sailing lessons but somehow never got around to it.

On the way down to the beach I picked up a stick and gave it a good throw, thinking that Brewster might want to play fetch. I should have known better. As usual, he stood there and looked at me, his head tilted quizzically to one side. It was as if he was thinking, "Why should I get it when you're the fool who threw it away? If you want it back, then you get it."

Rather than fetch worthless sticks thrown by stupid humans, Brewster preferred to spend his time in a more fruitful endeavor; in hot pursuit of the ocean, at least when the ocean wasn't in hot pursuit of him. When a wave rolled in he'd run up the beach just ahead of it, happily barking like a lunatic. When the wave receded, he'd turn around and chase it back to where it came from, still barking and proud of yet another triumph over the evil forces of nature.

After a few minutes, Dina asked, "So what's on your mind?"

"What makes you think something's on my mind?"

"Whenever you've got something you want to talk about, something that's pretty serious, you always suggest a walk on the beach," she explained.

"I can see we've been married too long," I said. "I need new tricks."

"Don't bother," she laughed. "They wouldn't work either. Besides, I kind of like your old tricks."

I told her about the meeting with Tolsa and Valencia. Stammering and fumbling, I explained that I'd agreed to team up with Valencia and find Tolsa's wife.

As I feared, she did not take it well.

"You did *what?*"

She didn't exactly shout, but she didn't exactly *not* shout either.

"I know it sounds a trifle trite, but you had to be there," I said feebly. "Tolsa's really hurting. I just couldn't turn him down, especially when Valencia said he'd go ahead with or without me, but he'd really like to have me with him."

That wasn't *exactly* what Valencia said. In fact, he didn't say that at all. But this was no time to clutter the issue with facts and accuracy.

"Correct me if I'm wrong, but isn't this kind of stuff they have police for?" she asked, sarcasm dripping like acid.

We were close to the water, where the sand was soft. Without warning, Dina angrily turned and stomped away, leaving deep footprints in the wet sand. Oddly, I could swear I heard her stifle a giggle, though I knew she was anything but in a laughing mood.

"Dina?" I asked, talking to her back. "Are you okay?"

"Hell, no, I'm not okay." She made that same strange choking noise. "What do you expect?"

As I hurried to catch up, I saw her shoulders heave. "Oh, God," I thought. "She's crying." I hate it when that happens. It's the ultimate weapon; the atomic bomb of emotional discourse.

Which was when she burst out laughing.

"Oh, goddammit!" she shouted, kicking hard at the sand.

"Okay, what's going on?" I asked, feeling like I was trapped in some kind of weird alternate universe. "I seem to have missed something."

"I bet Valencia that I could keep a straight face, act like I was angry, and make you feel guilty."

She finally turned around, a wide smile etched across her deceitful little beamer.

"But I couldn't even do it for five seconds, much less five minutes."

"What are … how …," I stammered.

She came back to me, stood on her toes, and gave me a kiss on the cheek.

"VALENCIA ALREADY TOLD me all about it," she said. "He came by the office early this morning, before Tolsa sent his messenger to you. He didn't know everything yet, but he knew enough to explain what he thought Tolsa wanted and said that if I objected he'd keep Tolsa from contacting you. If I was okay with it then he'd let it go ahead and play out. Whether you accepted was up to you, but he wanted to be sure I was all right with it first."

By now my jaw had dropped to the sand between my toes. I could tell that Dina was feeling contrite - although not nearly contrite enough, as far as I was concerned -

and was having second thoughts about her little trick. I let her feel that way. It was the least she deserved.

"Anyway, when I said that whatever you felt that you needed to do was okay with me and I probably couldn't stop you even if I wanted to, we made a bet that I couldn't act like I was mad when you told me, assuming you agreed to do it," she explained. "He said I'd crack and give it away. I told him I could hold it together for as long as I had to. Looks like I lost, dammit."

"*You* are a lizard, young lady," I declared. "As for Valencia, he's a deceitful Mexican twerp. I'll moida da bum. And you ...."

Giggling like idiots, we held each other as the sea water sloshed around our ankles.

"I knew you'd probably say 'yes'," she said, her head cradled next to my chest. "I mean, this *is* what you do, after all. Maybe it's time we stopped trying to pretend that it isn't and you're going to work in a gift shop and sell tacky sombreros with lots of cheap silver on them, or something."

"How much was the bet?"

"Twenty dollars."

"Twenty dollars! I bellowed, causing several nearby sea birds to take flight. "Do you know what twenty dollars will buy?"

She stood on tiptoe again, only this time she stuck her tongue in my ear.

"A good time, sailor boy?" she whispered.

"Not at today's rates," I said. "I was thinking about one of those cool sombreros."

"Boy, are you out of touch," she said. "They cost a lot more than twenty bucks."

"What about the good time?" I asked.

"The price just went up that, too," she said.

CHAPTER 12

WHEN WE GOT BACK to the house I called Chango Suarez in San Diego.

Tolsa's comment about O'Reilly's "radical" associates made me think that he might have a reputation or a sheet somewhere on either side of the border, although I had the feeling that what Tolsa regarded as radical I might consider middle of the road. If O'Reilly did, and if any of it spilled over into Southern California, Chango would either know about it or could find out easy enough.

Roberto "Chango" Suarez could have been chief of police years ago but wanted no part of the politics that went with the job. He was happy being a lieutenant. The rank gave him clout, but it wasn't high enough that it buried him in administrative baloney.

They still told the story of how, as a rookie beat cop, Chango and his partner interrupted a jewelry store robbery. The partner was shot as he got out of the patrol car. Chango killed two men, wounded a third, and somehow kept his partner alive even though he took one in the chest himself. He was back on the street in three months.

Chango would break any rule he pleased, but he had

his standards, even if nobody but him knew exactly what they were. He was happily married with 10 grown kids. Three were cops, four were lawyers, and the others were still in college, as far as I knew. The only time I saw the whole Suarez mob was at his yearly paella fest. He invited practically everybody he knew to his house where he made big drums of paella in the back yard. Crowds of people would come and go all day long while beer and wine flowed like a mighty river.

He was profane, tougher than Mount Everest, and always wore an ugly brown suit with a matching ugly brown tie. I didn't know if he had one suit that he wore everyday, or owned a closet full of the hideous things.

He picked up the phone on the second ring.

"Suarez."

"Chango, it's Ethan Cruickshank."

"Cruickshank? I thought you were in Mexico."

"I am. I'm calling from Cabo San Lucas. I need your help on something."

"Jesus H. Christ! Are you telling me you're back in business?" he asked.

"Yeah, I guess so."

"Are you sure that's a good idea?"

"Your confidence is inspiring," I said. "I'm touched."

"Yeah, you are, but probably not in the way you mean," he said.

I told him everything I new about the Tolsa kidnapping and everything that happened so far, including what Tolsa told us about Bernardo O'Reilly.

"That's pretty thin," he said.

"When thin is all there is, it looks pretty fat."

"Were you saving that, or something," he said.

"Nope," I said. "Spur of the moment."

"You know, I kind of like it. I might use it myself sometime."

"Bernardo O'Reilly," I said, getting back on track.

"What makes you think I know him?"

"I'm not saying you do. But it's a pretty unusual name. If you've ever run into the guy I thought you might remember it. Or maybe somebody else does. Or maybe he has a sheet somewhere."

"Somewhere?" he said. "You always were a pain in the ass."

All things considered, I thought it went pretty well.

CHAPTER 13

CHANGO CALLED BACK 45 minutes later.

"That was fast," I said.

"Everybody knows how much I like to drop everything to do you favors," he said.

"And the result of the latest one is?"

"I know him, or knew him. I had it with the name, but I wanted to check it out."

"Talk to me, Chango," I said.

"He's political, or used to me. Anarchist or socialist, or some bullshit. Somehow or another, he got involved with the gangs up here, but got out pretty quick. Drugs aren't his thing. He's not in it – whatever he thinks it is - for the money, at least not only for the money. I think he wants to save the world. Plus, he likes the action."

"You almost sound like you like him," I said.

"I do, or I did, kind of. There's something about him. He's a big, good-looking guy who knows how to handle himself and there are some things he won't do."

"How long ago did you know him?"

"Two or three years, probably closer to three."

"Anything else?"

"He's from La Paz down near your way. Still got

family there. Went to the university there, too. Don't know if he graduated, but I'd bet he didn't. My impression is that he kind of flits around without focus. Never really finishes anything, know what I mean?"

"Did he have a beard, by any chance?" I asked, thinking of Lilly's description of the leader.

"Yeah, he did. Probably thinks he's Che Guevera."

"You don't have a photograph, do you?"

"Nobody does, that I know of. He was always careful about that. Smart."

"Thanks, Chango. I owe you."

"Yeah, but you never pay up. What are you gonna do now?"

"Probably just blunder around like I always do."

CHAPTER 14

THE RESTAURANT where I agreed to meet Valencia the next morning was a hole in the wall with an open front just off Cabo's little town square. I got there before Valencia did, took a table on the patio, and ordered a heap of *huevos rancheros* with a side of well-done hash browns, toast, and orange juice. Valencia showed up ten minutes later and ordered a muffin and coffee.

"You don't eat enough," I said. "You drink too much coffee, too."

Valencia put a manila file folder on the table and looked at my breakfast with withering disdain.

"And you must be on the Henry the Eighth diet" He gestured disdainfully at my plate. "If that's what you usually eat for breakfast then you will be dead in about a week."

"I don't do this every day," I replied. "But since you're paying I figured I might as well get the full ride. You *did* win a small fortune from my wife."

Valencia grinned broadly at the news.

"I didn't think she could hold out."

He opened one of those little butter patties wrapped

inside the usual hard-to-unfold paper and spread it over half of his muffin.

"If I'm paying for breakfast, then where are my winnings?" he asked.

"I'm not responsible for my wife's gambling debts," I said. "Your bet was with her, so you collect from her."

"I'll probably never see it," he said with a shrug. "I know how you gringos operate, how you take advantage of the natives when you're not trying to kill them."

"It's worked pretty well for us so far," I agreed. "So how'd you're research go? Mine turned out better than I expected. O'Reilly might be our horse after all."

I told him what I'd learned from Chango. Valencia nodded as he took a bite of his muffin.

"Yes, Bernardo O'Reilly looks like a possibility," he agreed. "Of course, right now he's the only possibility. I checked every law enforcement and government database I could access in Mexico, Guatemala, Panama, Costa Rica, and the United States, plus Interpol. I spoke with several of Tolsa's employees, too."

"I didn't realize we were dealing with an international criminal mastermind," I joked. "That's a helluva night's work. I'm surprised you didn't go blind staring at the computer that long."

I shoveled a forkful of *huevos rancheros* in my mouth, chewed lightly, and washed it down with orange juice. A female tourist who was shaped like a badly-packed sandbag and wearing cutoff jeans, a t-shirt, and a straw hat that might have cost as much as three dollars stopped on the sidewalk about ten feet away and watched me eat as if I were a local attraction she'd paid good money to see. I gave her a friendly wave with my fork as if I was the king and the fork was my scepter. Her eyes widened and she hurried away.

"It's good to be the king," I said.

"*Que?*" Valencia asked.

"Mel Brooks in *A History of the World, Part II*," I said.

"Class," he sighed. "Nothing but class. My country is so lucky to have you."

I took another bite of my eggs, followed by another swallow of orange juice, and pushed my chair back from the table.

"My guess is that a captain with the Cabo San Lucas police department is not supposed to have access to a lot of the information you have in that folder," I said. "At least not in the way you probably got it."

"That's the rumor." Valencia shrugged.

"So much for crack internet security," I said.

Valencia patted the folder. "O'Reilly has an interesting background. As your man said, he seems to suffer from the cause-of-the-month syndrome. It might be easier to list the organizations he *hasn't* joined over the years than those he has."

"What kind of organizations?"

"Generally environmental and political, most of them with occasional, and sometimes more than occasional, forays into illegality."

Valencia took a sip of coffee and another bite of muffin, leaving me to ponder what "forays into illegality" was supposed to mean.

"As your friend said, Bernardo O'Reilly was born in La Paz," Valencia said. "He comes from a large family; five brothers and six sisters, although two sisters and one brother died of natural causes when they were very young. He attended the university there, taking mostly liberal arts courses like philosophy and history, although he never graduated. You'll be interested to know that a young woman named Maria Torres attended the university at the same time. She later married and her name became Maria Tolsa."

"Now *there's* a nifty little nugget," I said. "So this obsession, if that's what it is, probably goes back a lot further than Tolsa thinks, assuming it exists at all."

"Exactly," Valencia agreed.

"Did they know each other then?" I asked.

"Impossible to say," Valencia replied. "They have no organizations in common that I could find."

"What else did you learn?"

"Through the years, O'Reilly was associated with several groups that have the goal of saving everything from the whales to the rain forest, some of them quite militant. Other groups to which he belonged have no intention of saving anything but themselves while fattening their wallets. The information is a little vague at times, but he appears to have been a fringe member of the Zapatista rebel group. The Zapatistas' cause was Indian rights, particularly in Chiapas. He may have been peripherally involved with MS-13, which was originally known as the *Mara Salvatrucha* street gang. It was formed in Los Angeles, then took root here after most of the key members were deported to Mexico and Central America, where it thrived thanks to a large recruiting pool of disaffected young people. Now MS-13 operates everywhere from El Salvador to the United States, a dangerous gang involved in everything from human smuggling and narcotics trafficking to document forgery. A long string of murders is linked to MS-13, too. O'Reilly's involvement was out of character for him, not particularly heavy, and he seems to have dropped out after a short time. That's his pattern. Whatever it is, he stays for a while, until he becomes disillusioned or bored, and then moves on."

My *huevos rancheros* were only half eaten, but I was already full. Despite Valencia's gibe, Henry VIII would have done better by them.

"So what we may have here is an idealist who's

constantly disappointed but ever hopeful," I said. "He's a wannabe revolutionary who can't find the right revolution and pulls out when things get either too serious or not serious enough. He wants to be Che Guevera but without the getting killed part."

"Perhaps," Valencia agreed. "That's a common enough creature, except that they're usually harmless and even rather silly. They usually grow out of it. At some point, they figure out that saving the world doesn't pay well. At any rate, as you might guessed, O'Reilly's had many brushes with the law, although he was never charged with anything hard. He is comfortable with firearms and spent time around people and groups responsible for a variety of complex operations over the years, many of them violent. Some successful and some not."

"Including kidnapping?"

"Including kidnapping, although, as far as I could tell O'Reilly was never directly involved. He seems to never have been directly involved with anything of significance. It's as if he's there and yet not there at the same time."

"Maybe he's a watcher and not a doer?" I said. "Or maybe he's too smart to leave tracks and gets out when he either gets what he wants or before things get too hot? Anyway, it fits pretty well, doesn't it, especially since we don't have anything else?"

Valencia waved to the waitress for more coffee.

"Did you find anything on O'Reilly after Tolsa fired him?" I asked.

"Apparently he went back to La Paz, back to the mother ship, you might say," Valencia said. "He charged some gasoline there with a false card he's used before. That was more than a year ago. Whether he is still there is impossible to tell, although there is no record of him being anywhere else, not that there necessarily would be such a thing. He could be anywhere, including right here."

"No work or payroll records?" I asked.

"No, but he can always work for cash," he said. "As Tolsa said, many here do."

"You have last-known addresses for the surviving members of his family, right" I asked.

Valencia just smiled.

"Silly me, of course you do," I said. "So it looks like we're going to La Paz."

"I have an idea about that," Valencia said. "I would like to have some cover."

"How do you mean?"

When he explained what he meant I almost wished that I hadn't asked.

"You want to go to La Paz with Nicole and Lilly? In their camper? The four of us?"

"Think about it," he explained. "They're professionals and having them with us would double our manpower. The cover is ideal. We'd be two couples sightseeing in La Paz, not two men asking a lot of questions. We would still ask the questions, but we wouldn't be so noticeable."

I had to admit that it wasn't a bad idea, although it promised to be a little awkward.

"We will need one more vehicle, I think," Valencia said. "Something we can tow behind the camper."

"I'm sure you already have one in mind," I grumbled, still not sure about the Lilly and Nicole idea.

"As a matter of fact, I do," he said. "I have a cousin who has something that should fit our needs perfectly."

Valencia always had "a cousin." They seemed to be stashed all over the country and magically able to supply whatever he needed whenever he needed it. I envied that. Most of my relatives were just a pain in the butt.

"You know, Lilly and Nicole won't do it for love," I said. "They may not do it at all. In their place, I don't think I would."

"I'm not sure I would either," Valencia admitted. "On the other hand, I'm sure Tolsa will make it worth their while."

"Still, if I had to bet my feeling is that they might go for it, Lilly especially" I admitted. "Call it a working vacation."

CHAPTER 15

THE DREAM CAME THAT NIGHT, the same as all the other dreams of so many other nights.

It was as if I was watching from somewhere high up in my parents' bedroom. But, at the same time, I could see myself, the half-asleep five-year-old who innocently walked down the hall into the horror that would change his life.

I said something as I stepped into the room, although I couldn't hear it. There was no sound in my dream. There never was. But the me who was watching knew that the other me – the scared little boy in pajamas – had cried out for his mom and dad.

There were two men standing at my father's side of the bed. They both had baseball bats with the barrels resting on their shoulders, like they were waiting to take batting practice. In the dream, neither man had features, or even a face. They were just there.

They turned in the little boy's direction when they heard him say something. The closest one was tall and skinny, with purple tattoos covering his pale hairless forearms. He lifted one hand off the knob at the bottom of the bat, took a half-step, and swept his arm backhand in a long arc. I saw the back of his hand hit the little boy that was me on the side of the head. The man didn't look very strong, but the boy was small and the blow lifted him off his feat as he bounced off the bedroom wall and collapsed in a heap. It didn't really hurt. There was no pain as he laid there with his eyes wide open and his head cradled against the baseboard, terribly afraid in the one place in the world where he should have felt safest.

My mother screamed. In my dream she made no sound, but the watching me knew that she screamed, her mouth forming an almost perfect oval. She threw the covers off and started to come to her little boy, but my father pushed her down with one hand as he shot out of the bed with a wild snarl, fighting to protect his wife and son. He was strong and his hands closed tight around the throat of the man who hit me. Although I still couldn't hear anything, I knew that my father was making a strange roaring sound, like an enraged animal. They fell to the ground with my father on top, his hands cinched around the skinny man's throat while *his* fingers desperately clawed at my father's back.

The other man was short and stocky with thick heavy arms. He lifted the baseball bat over his head like it was an ax and he was splitting logs for firewood. It happened so fast the eye shouldn't have been able to follow, but the watching me saw the bat as it moved toward the back of my father's head with terrible killing power ....

I heard a scream. This time it was me, the real me, but it was the little boy, too. Dina saved me from the dream with a hand on my shoulder and a gentle kiss on my cheek.

I was balled into the fetal position. My breath came in hard gasps and I could feel my heart pounding in my chest like something trying to beat down the door of a dungeon. Dina slid one arm under my shoulder and wrapped the other arm around me, holding me tight against her.

"It's all right, Ethan. Everything is all right," she whispered. "I'm here with you, we're at home, and everything's okay."

I didn't move from her embrace. My heart was thumping and my body was clammy with fear.

"It was the dream again." My voice was hoarse and trembling. "The same one."

"I know," she whispered, her lips caressing my ear. "Just stay here with me and it'll all go away. You'll be all right. Just hold on to me, Ethan. Hold on tight."

Although the details varied, the dream always stopped at the same place. Sometimes Dina woke me up, and sometimes I woke myself, but it never went any further. I never saw the blow land, and all the blows that must have come after that. But up to that point I saw what happened and I was part of it at the same time. The psychiatrists told me that the dream might be worse than the real thing because I knew what was going to happen and couldn't stop it.

Did it really happen that way? No one could say for sure, not even me.

I straightened my legs, turned over wrapped my arms around Dina, and we held each other so I could I surround myself with the protection of her love.

I did not go back to sleep that night. I don't think she did either. It was always that way. I was saved, but the little boy had to stay where he was, trapped in a nightmare for all eternity.

CHAPTER 16

WE DIDN'T TALK about it in the morning. Maybe it would have been better if we did. Talking about it is supposed to be good. But we'd been through it so often that there wasn't anything left to say that hadn't already been said so many times that I was sick of it. I'd long ago grown tired of being so self-absorbed and having to take my own temperature all the time.

As expected, Lilly and Nicole agreed to go to La Paz. Valencia called to say that they'd pick me up at ten. Instead of waiting around and worrying, Dina decided to go to work.

"Saying goodbye is icky enough," she explained. "I don't want to do it in front of strangers."

We held each other close and kissed hard.

"You be sure and call me," she said.

"Damn right I'll call you," I said. "Every day."

Dina was taking Brewster with her so he wouldn't go berserk at the sight of strangers approaching, or, God forbid, actually in his house. He wouldn't do anything but bark, but Lilly and Nicole didn't know that. Dina opened the passenger door of her Mercedes, made a little clicking sound, and he happily jumped in. Sitting in the passenger's seat, he was taller than Dina when she got behind the wheel. He thought that going to work with her was just about the coolest thing in the universe. For some reason, he was always perfectly calm when someone walked into her office. Maybe it was because he didn't feel that he had to defend his home turf, but there he was a different dog.

Looking at our boy sitting upright and raring to go, I said, "It looks like he's not much for those long drawn-out goodbyes either."

"He's a sensible little man," she said. "We raised him well."

I leaned into the car and kissed her again. We said all the dumb things that come when people don't know what to say.

"See you, kid."

"You take care of yourself."

"Don't worry. This'll probably be a wild goose chase. There's a pretty good chance that we'll come back in a few days kind of embarrassed and wondering why we went in the first place."

I stepped back while she started the Mercedes, wheeled it around and drove away, tires crunching on the gravel. She turned left on the highway and gave me a wave and a goodbye honk. I waited until she was out of sight before walking back into the house.

My head felt gummy from lack of sleep. I was tempted to take a short nap but a glance at the clock told me there wasn't enough time because I still had to pack.

I am not the world's greatest packer and this trip was hard to calibrate because I didn't know how long I'd be gone. Fortunately, I wasn't walking to La Paz with everything on my back, so I could take the kitchen sink if I felt like it.

Not the least of my decisions involved firearms. I

don't consider myself a collector, but over the years I've accumulated a dozen pieces ranging from a twenty-caliber Beretta I use when I need an ankle piece to a beautiful Webley and Scott twelve gauge shotgun. Built in Birmingham, England, it's a forty-year-old hand-engraved knockout, with twenty-eight inch barrels.

After hefting one piece after the other, I decided to take my trusty old SIG P210, a nine millimeter with a walnut grip. It was almost thirty years old and the magazine only held eight rounds, but it was the most accurate and reliable weapon I'd ever used. It never let me down.

I wanted something with a lot of stopping power, too, just in case. I probably wouldn't need it, but it would be better to have it and not need it than to need it and not have it. The problem was that we'd be dressing light to fit in and if all I had on was a bathing suit and a t-shirt lugging around something the size of a Colt Python might be a giveaway that I was not just another tourist taking in the sights of La Paz.

I decided on my Colt Officer's ACP with an aluminum alloy frame. It was a forty five that would drop anything short of a charging moose, but it only weighed twenty four ounces, which was less than the SIG weighed. Like the SIG, with only six shots the capacity was a little light, but we weren't headed to the OK Corral. I crammed everything into one suitcase and one soft lambskin bag, including my reading material. I had finished Michael Palin and had moved on to David McCullough's "1776."

It seemed like I heard the rumble of the big Dodge diesel about ten minutes for before it showed up. It pulled up in front of the house and I walked outside with my bags and locked the door.

It wasn't until I took in the full picture that I saw what was being towed behind the camper – an aged and incredibly gnarly-looking jeep of most uncertain vintage. In fact, everything about it was pretty uncertain. It looked like it was left over from Patton's march across Europe during World War II. Two of the fenders had been replaced and because no one bothered to paint them the colors didn't match the rest of the faded green vehicle. With one light blue and one black, the fenders didn't even match each other, which didn't particularly matter because the rest of the jeep looked like a tribute to Bondo. With patches of the stuff here, there, and everywhere, it looked like a bad rash. Even with all the patching, there were several places where rust continued to do its slow but deadly work.

All told, the thing resembled a quilt on wheels, a really old and raggedy quilt partially eaten by rats.

Valencia climbed down from the passenger side of the truck.

"Is *that* your idea of the perfect vehicle?" I asked. "Your cousin was probably glad to get rid of it."

"Trust me, it will fit right in," he said, resolutely ignoring my skepticism. "No one will ever notice it. It might as well be invisible."

"Unfortunately, it's not," I said.

Despite my grousing, Valencia was right. It would be great camouflage. In its way, that pile of junk was a microcosm of everything that was wrong - and right - with Mexico. It was only recently that the country developed a middle class of any significance. Even now, most of the people are either very well off or very poor, with the poor being much in the majority. They run their cars and trucks until they die an ugly death, cannibalizing parts from other cars along the way as needed. While their transportation looks like hell, the owners squeeze every last mile out of every last part, which probably wouldn't be a bad habit for the rest of the world to adopt.

When a vehicle finally goes to that great car lot in the sky, as often as not the owner simply coasts to the side of the road and walks away, leaving what's left to be stripped down to the shell by anybody who needs what working parts they can salvage.

There's something about an abandoned car that I always find irresistible. When everybody else sees an eyesore, I see … who the hell knows? It's hard to explain.

I remember discovering an abandoned car in a big empty field across the street from our house when I was a boy. I was so awed by it I came back every day for the next two weeks. To this day, I don't know what make of car it was, or how it got there, but that didn't matter. The old heap seemed full of mystery and wonderful but vague possibilities that I was too young to articulate. I can still feel the sharp hurt of disappointment when it wasn't there one morning. I heard later that somebody complained and the city hauled it away. Its sudden disappearance hurt so bad I wanted to cry. I probably did.

Yes, Valencia was right, an ugly wreck like this one would fit in perfectly, no doubt about it.

The Dodge Ram had a huge cab, with plenty of room for all four of us. Feeling like a mountain goat, I climbed up and into the truck. Nicole drove, with Valencia next to her. Lilly and I took the back seat.

"So what made you two decide to come, other than my friend's golden tongue, his fine taste in transportation, and money?" I asked.

After a moment of silence, Lilly replied, "I liked the manager."

"You mean Hernandez; the guy who got killed at *El Campeador*?"

"They didn't have to kill him," she said. "He seemed like a good guy."

"They probably didn't have to kill the three guards at

Tolsa's place either," I agreed. "The whole operation was a lot bloodier than it had to be."

Valencia threw his arm over the seat so he could face us.

"It was excessive, I agree, but that's not as unusual," he explained. "Dead men can't give descriptions and they can't identify anyone. They're just dead."

"They didn't have to kill the manager," Lilly stubbornly repeated. "I still don't like it."

"Yeah, I don't either," Nicole said.

"That probably makes it unanimous," I said, snuggling down in the seat. I intended to take a nap. Last night was pretty rocky.

CHAPTER 17

ALTHOUGH THE DRIVE to La Paz was as uneventful as it was beautiful, I didn't sleep more than a few minutes.

Southern Baja's true nature took over a few minutes after we left Cabo San Lucas, driving through an austere and mostly uninhabited landscape of desert and sea. The barren hills and mountains on our right were studded with forests of giant Cardon cacti that tumbled down to the shore on our left. Throughout most of Baja, the lush tropical vegetation that tourists see is almost always man-made. It needs to be planted, replanted, watered, and constantly nurtured. Living in Cabo, with all its emerald golf courses, it's easy to forget about the time, money, and effort it takes to keep them looking that way.

For lunch, we pulled off the two-lane highway and drove a short way down a rutted dirt road to a deserted stretch of beach where we feasted on a batch of tamales Valencia brought with him. I refused a beer. Drinking beer in the afternoon makes me sleepy. On some days that's not a bad thing, but today I opted for bottled iced tea.

When we finished lunch and resumed the drive,

passing the artists' colony of Todos Santos on the way, Valencia asked, "Have any of you ever been to La Paz?"

"A couple of times, but only briefly," I replied. "I don't know it well. Just the main stuff."

Lilly and Nicole knew even less than I did. They'd changed places at lunch and now Lilly was driving and Nicole was in the back seat with me.

"We passed it on the way down, but didn't stop," Nicole explained. "According to the guide books, there isn't a lot there for tourists anyway."

"That's probably true for most tourists, but La Paz is a very pleasant town, one that's well worth seeing," Valencia said. "Although it's the capital of *Baja California Sur*, and approaching two hundred thousand people, it has the charm of a smaller city. It's on a wide bay off the Sea of Cortez and the *malecon* – the sea wall boulevard - follows the twisting shoreline through town. On one side of the *malecon* there are shops, restaurants and a few hotels. On the other side there is a wide sidewalk flanked by coconut palms and the beach. The city seems smaller than it is because most of the buildings are only two or three stories, so there are no high rises to disrupt the flow of sky, hills, and sea. No matter where you are along the *malecon*, it's just a few steps to the water, although the best beaches are outside of town."

Valencia looked around to see if he was boring us with his travelogue. He never said it in so many words, but I knew that he loved the beauty and diversity of his country, even though he was all too aware of Mexico's many problems, and enjoyed talking about it when he was in the mood. We encouraged him to continue.

"The Spanish came to the area in the early fifteen hundreds, at about the same time they came to *Los Cabos*. Most of them were Cortez's men lusting after the world's finest pink and black pearls. Two hundred years later it was the Jesuits' turn. In addition to Christianity, these soldiers of Christ brought the smallpox that wiped out most of the Indian population. Gradually the area became a haven for people who were desperate to get away from the endless revolutions on the mainland, as one government toppled another year after year. When a virus killed the oyster beds in the nineteen forties, that killed the pearl business, too, and La Paz was left isolated and alone. Although it's fairly well-known for its fishing and diving, the city has no other major attractions so it's not flooded by tourists, although there are several good hotels and a two or three large resorts outside of town. I understand that more are on the way. Englebert Humperdinck once owned a resort there."

"Did I just hear you say Englebert Humperdinck?" I said.

Valencia grinned. "I'm afraid so."

"If anybody starts singing 'Please, Release Me' I'll shoot them," I said.

I should have kept my mouth shut. Lilly launched into a terrible, and mercifully brief, rendition, which wasn't helped by the fact that she didn't know the words after the first verse. She sounded like her fingernails were being slowly pulled out one at a time. Once we stopped laughing, we had to beg Valencia to continue, as long as he promised not to bring up Englebert Hunperdinck again.

"The *Isla Espiritu Santo* off the coast is the best-known island in Baja," he said. "It's actually two big islands, plus several smaller rock outcroppings, with at least a dozen white sandy beaches. You can visit a sea lion colony or go diving among tropical fish in almost crystal clear water. Because La Paz does not rank high as a tourist attraction, the pace of life is much slower than in the resort cities. The open-air terrace of the old Perla Hotel on the *malecon* is a popular place for the locals to sit and watch the world go by. The old men of the town stay there for hours at a time, and the *malecon* itself becomes alive at night."

"You should go to work for the tourist bureau," Lilly said. "How do you know so much about the place?"

"I was born there," Valencia replied.

"Like Bernardo O'Reilly?" Nicole asked.

"Like Bernardo O'Reilly," he said.

"Is your family still there?"

"I am the last of my family."

"Speaking of family, where does O'Reilly's family live, assuming they're still there?" I asked.

"In town a few blocks from the *malecon*," Valencia replied. "It's nothing exceptional, a house like many others."

"Is there a convenient place somewhere nearby where we can park this rig for a few days and not be noticed?" Lilly asked.

"That will be easy," Valencia explained. "There are a number of places, particularly along the beach, that offer the combination of isolation and convenience we want."

"Depending on how long we stay, it might be good to move from place to place so our movements won't fall into a pattern," I said. "You know, a night or two here, a night or two there."

"Golly gee, you must be a trained investigator," Nicole said. "Just think, I'm on a road trip with Dick Tracy."

"The obvious is my specialty," I replied.

"We could move around, as you suggest, but I don't think it will be necessary, at least not that often," Valencia said.

We rolled into La Paz and slowly drove along the *malecon* so that Nicole, Lilly and I could get oriented. There wasn't much traffic and it only took about ten minutes. Once we passed through town we pulled into a Pemex station to get some diesel for the truck. Valencia and I jumped out of the truck as an attendant wearing a greasy brown jump suit with the Pemex logo over the chest pocket approached the Dodge. Valencia seized one arm, pulled him aside, and got in his face with a lot of finger wagging while I folded my arms across my chest and looked menacing. After much waving of hands and protestations of innocence, the attendant sullenly gave in and returned to the dumpy little shack that passed as an office. He did something under the counter and then waved at us to pump our own gas. Once we finished, he came out, took our money, returned the change, turned on his heel and went back inside, all without making eye contact.

"What was that all about?" Lilly asked as we pulled out of the station.

"*Litros incompletos*," I replied.

"Incomplete liters?" Nicole asked. "What's that supposed to mean?"

"Short liters," I said. "They do it all over Mexico. Not everywhere and not all the time, but often enough that you have to watch for it."

"The pumps are rigged so that you don't get all the gasoline you pay for," Valencia explained. "All gas stations in Mexico are franchises of our state-owned oil company, *Petroleos Mexicanos* …."

" … otherwise known as Pemex," I continued. "The government sets the price but it's easy for the station people - the *gasolineros* - rig the pumps to goose their profits."

"Did you see when he went back inside and reached underneath the counter?" asked Valencia. "He pushed a reset button to restore the equipment so that it would dispense full liters. Once we left he pressed it again to dispense the usual short liters."

"How do you know he just didn't fake it and we still got short liters?" Lilly asked.

"Because Valencia told him that he would come back and cut off his *cojones* if he found out we were short-pumped," I said.

"That might do it," said Nicole.

With our tank now full, we turned back the way we came and started our search for a place to stay. We rejected two spots before coming to a place Valencia knew about, one that was his first choice all along. It was a mile and a half south of town. Judging by the small pile of ashes ringed by a circle of rocks, it wasn't exactly a secret. Still, it seemed ideal. We were on the beach in a small cove, but couldn't be seen from the road, thanks to the scrubby trees and cactus and the way the land rose from the beach. The crisp earthy smell of the ocean was strong in the air. On either side of the cove, the curving beach stretched until it disappeared into the mist. In the far distance, the sea and the sky seemed to blend together so that it was impossible to tell when one stopped and the other started.

The only sign of human life was a solitary old man who was surf fishing about a quarter of a mile away. He'd either walked in, or his vehicle was parked somewhere down the beach where we couldn't see it.

The camper was self-contained, including a generator. According to Lilly and Nicole, as long as nobody lingered too long under the shower it would be several days before we'd have to leave, find a hookup somewhere, empty all the gunge out, and re-supply.

Sweating and cursing, Valencia and I struggled to disengage the old jeep from the rear of the camper while

Nicole and Lilly did the same thing with the truck in front of the camper. They had a lot more practice and finished well ahead of us, but without the sweating and cursing. We opened the awning, put the picnic table and chairs outside, and pushed the camper's side extension out.

In less than thirty minutes, our little operation was open for business. There was just one more thing to be resolved – the sleeping arrangements.

Lilly took charge of that one.

"Nikky and I will take the bed." She glared at us as if we'd challenged her. "Why, you ask? Because it's our camper, that's why."

"It never occurred to me to think otherwise," Valencia said, his eyes shining with amusement.

"One of you can sleep in the sofa bed," Lilly continued. "It's too small for two men to sleep in it and actually get any sleep. Even if it wasn't, being such manly bastards I doubt that you'd both want to sleep in it anyway."

We looked at the sofa bed, looked at each other, and shook our heads. Manly bastards R us.

"Whoever doesn't sleep there can sleep in the cabin," she said. "It's more comfortable than it looks. I've slept there plenty of times. So has Nikky. The only problem comes when you've got to go to the can in the middle of the night. The upside is that if any of us snore, you won't have to hear it."

Valencia I flipped a coin. I called heads and lost, which meant I got the cabin.

"Oh, what the hell," I shrugged. "I once spent a week on a case sleeping in the back seat of a Chevy Chevette. By the time it was over, I needed a chiropractor. Compared to that, this'll be downright spacious."

"You can try all you want to make lemonade out of lemons," Valencia scoffed. "But I know who won, gringo, and it wasn't you."

CHAPTER 18

THE NEXT MORNING we went looking for Bernardo O'Reilly.

The best address we had for his family was five or six blocks in from the *malecon*. Like most traditional Mexican houses, it was set flush on the sidewalk, made of the same earth-colored stucco over cinder block that was popular all over Baja. The house looked like a couple of child's blocks placed one on top of the other. The bottom block was horizontal while the top block was vertical and covered only about half the bottom level. There was a one-vehicle car port on the right side of the house. The front windows and door were arched. The street was paved with concrete and had not been well maintained by the city, or maintained at all. The big uneven cracks resembled leftover damage from an earthquake. A one-story house was on the right side of the O'Reilly place, with an empty lot with tall and flourishing weeds and a fascinating variety of trash on the left. With no alley to separate one street from the next, the neighborhood lots backed up to each other. Unless you were willing to ramble through the back neighbor's yard, which meant climbing over a cinder block wall that was eight feet high, the front was the only way in or out. The rest of the street was a dodgy mix of residential and rundown commercial, with what looked like apartments over the shops. The shops were a break. With more people coming and going than on a typical residential street, it would be harder for somebody to spot us watching the place.

We drove past the house one way and then turned around and came back. To our disappointment, Maria Tolsa did not appear at a window and cry for help.

"According to the property records, the family has owned this house for almost forty years," Valencia said. "O'Reilly probably was raised there."

One part of our brilliant plan was to watch the house in six-hour shifts. The other part was to creep the house to see what we could find. A clue would be nice.

We watched for a day to figure out the pattern of whoever lived there. I was first, followed by Lilly, Valencia, and Nicole. After the first twenty four hours, we'd vary the order and alternate between the truck and the jeep so that no one in the neighborhood would get used to seeing any of us or our transportation at a specific time.

I always hated this part of the work because it was so damn boring. Knowing we'd be in for some surveillance, I'd packed the standard gear: binoculars, a camera with short, medium and long lenses, spare batteries for the camera, a notebook, pens, pencils, a flashlight with extra batteries, and two different kinds of sunglasses, one pair of Ray-Ban aviators and a pair of blue wrap-around Oakleys that made me look like Batman. I had two hats, too. One was a Dodgers baseball cap. The other was a straw riverboat gambler's hat Dina bought for me years ago up in Carmel. She said it was the only hat I'd ever worn that didn't make me look like a dork. I didn't know whether to be insulted or pleased. The two hats and two pair of sunglasses gave me several different looks. The precautions probably weren't necessary, but it's always better to take them.

Before my shift, I loaded a thermos full of ice chips, too. On more kinds of surveillance than I could remember, I found that ice chips quenched my thirst without filling my bladder.

Speaking of my bladder, before heading out I tossed an empty half-gallon milk carton on the jeep's passenger-side floor. TV and movie private detectives on surveillance must have bladders the size of Pluto because finding a bathroom is never a consideration. In real life, when you've gotta go, you've really gotta go and an empty half-gallon milk carton makes a dandy receptacle. The trick is to be alert to your surroundings. It's not sound sleuthing practice to relieve yourself just as somebody's gray-haired Aunt Martha strolls past the car.

I parked down the block and on the other side of the street from the house, far enough away that I wouldn't be noticed unless someone was looking for me, but close enough so that I could see the front door. I'd also move the Jeep a couple of times during my six-hour shift. The changes made me harder to spot and help alleviate boredom at the same time.

Everybody has a different approach to surveillance, especially from a parked car. I've known some PIs who listen to music through a set of headphones or an i-pod. Others read a book, presumably a lousy book so they won't get too engrossed, or listen to a book on tape or CD. I knew one guy who swore that he could detach his brain from his body. He'd get settled in and comfortable, then let his brain drift away from his surroundings until the person he was following reappeared and his brain snapped back in place. He claimed that it was a form of meditation.

None of that worked for me. When my brain detaches from my body I usually fall asleep, which wouldn't get me a bust in the private detective hall of fame. I tried music and reading and didn't like it. I was always afraid I'd miss something.

It was going to be a hot day but I couldn't run the air conditioner in the jeep because there wasn't any air conditioner to run. For a distraction, I could always think about how hot and uncomfortable I was.

As usual, the anticipation was the worst part. My shift wasn't that bad. Once I grew used to the surroundings, I spent most of the time running through the list of heavy-weight champions in my head, trying to figure out who would have beaten whom. I even took notes. After a while, I had my tournament down to Jack Johnson, Joe Louis, Mohammed Ali and Mike Tyson in his prime. Thanks to his superior jab, Louis was about to beat a bloody Tyson on a TKO in the tenth round when I was relieved by Lilly, who parked the truck a block down the other way on the same side of the street as the house.

She called me on her cell phone.

"How'd it go?"

"Smashing," I said. "You'll have gobs of fun. The time just flies by."

"You, sir, are a big fat liar," she said.

"I am *not* fat," I said.

CHAPTER 19

AFTER THE FIRST thirty six hours we had a fix on who lived in the house; three Mexican males with dark hair, mid-20s to mid-30s. One had a mustache while the other two were clean shaven. None of them seemed to have regular employment and none of them were Bernardo O'Reilly. Their shared transportation included one Honda motorcycle, one light gray Toyota SUV, and one battered Chevy truck that looked like it was almost as old as our jeep. Since we didn't know their names, we called them Tom, Dick and Harry, or, collectively, the guys.

Since there were long stretches when all three of them were out, it didn't seem likely that Maria Tolsa was inside the house, even if she was bound and gagged and chained to a bedpost. As a rule, kidnappers don't like to leave their meal ticket alone, especially when it's worth more than ten million dollars.

It was time to creep. Valencia and I would go in while Nicole watched from the street in case one of the guys came back to the house. Lilly was stationed a couple of blocks away to pick us up when we finished.

Given the set up, the only way to do it was to approach from the front and go around to the back door because the high wall in the back yard would give us some privacy while we cracked the lock.

The trick was to get in and out without leaving any sign we were there because we didn't want to alert the guys that they were being watched. Fortunately, I brought my kit with me and the lock was cheap. It only took about thirty seconds before we were inside the house. True, that was about fifteen seconds too long, but I was rusty.

We could tell no one was there the minute we opened the door. There's a peculiar stillness to an empty place that doesn't feel like anything else. As we entered, I felt a tingling in my groin, the same one I felt as a kid playing hide and seek. Some things don't change.

The house was pretty much what it seemed to be from the outside. We'd walked into a combination living and dining room. To one side was a small kitchen with a pass through into the dining room. Bedrooms and bathrooms were upstairs.

It was clear right away that the guys were not disciples of Martha Stewart. A lot of the furniture was early Salvation Army, and that was the good stuff. The beds were unmade and the sink was full of dirty dishes encrusted with remnants of meals past. A search of the kitchen wastebasket revealed nothing except that they were fond of bananas and badly needed to take the garbage out. The clothes hanging in the tiny bedroom closets upstairs were an exciting combination of cheap, gaudy and old.

A search of the bedroom dressers revealed that they all favored briefs over boxers and were not fans of natural fibers in men's hosiery. They smoked grass, too. I found a couple of ounces in a baggie hidden underneath some socks, next to a forty five Colt with a pearl handle grip. How tacky. I remembered a line from "Patton" about how only a pimp from a cheap New Orleans whorehouse would carry a gun with a pearl handle grip. Patton himself preferred ivory.

A look under the bed revealed nothing but a healthy family of dust bunnies. A search of the bathroom told us that Crest was their toothpaste of choice. Judging by the tangled pile of green floss in the bathroom wastebasket, somebody was scrupulous about dental hygiene. Dina was a dedicated flosser, too. I should floss, but I rarely did. It was too much trouble. Someday all my teeth would fall out and I'd have only myself to blame.

The shower featured a fascinating display of disgusting mold darkening the grout between the white tiles on the wall and along the bottom of the plastic curtain. The soap was a mess of congealed goo in the soap dish built into the tile.

There was a small cheap desk in one bedroom with a desktop computer on a stand next to it. After rummaging through the desk and finding nothing, Valencia turned on the computer and checked out the documents. The metal wastebasket next to the desk was so full that it overflowed. I dumped the contents on the floor and went through everything piece by piece, refilling the wastebasket as I went. I made the fascinating discovery that at least one of the guys chewed gum. But could he walk at the same time?

I was almost through with trash patrol when Valencia said, "Look what we have here." I rose to my feet, looked over his shoulder at the computer screen and beheld the ransom note. Valencia made a print-out, folded it in half and put it in his hip pocket. A few minutes more and we were ready to go. Before leaving the house, we did a walk through to make sure that we left everything exactly as we found it, even the trash.

Satisfied that the guys wouldn't know that anyone

had broken into their castle, we locked the door and walked around to the front of the house and down the street. I don't know about Valencia, but I had to fight my instinct to hurry. People might remember a couple of guys in a hurry. They probably wouldn't remember a couple of guys who looked like they belonged there and took their sweet time on the way to wherever they were going. Maybe they'd think we were from the phone company, or something? I found myself humming "Wichita Lineman" while Valencia called Lilly, who picked us up a couple of blocks down and one street over.

CHAPTER 20

WITH PROOF that we were on the right track, we agreed to change our plan; one of us would watch the house while the other three split up to follow the guys. Valencia and I increased our transportation to equal our needs by renting a couple of anonymous white compact Nissans at the La Paz airport.

After the first night, I changed my sleeping arrangement, too. Despite Lilly's endorsement, the truck cab was too hot and cramped, even with the windows down. It was like trying to sleep in a steaming tea bag. I bought a cheap chaise lounge in town and slept on the beach, wrapped in a blanket with a pillow under my head and lulled to sleep by the gentle sounds of the surf.

There shortly followed another change that involved the sleeping arrangement *inside* the camper. One night I went in to take a wiz and saw Lilly in her black pajamas, sprawled out on the sofa bed where Valencia was supposed to be. The door to the bedroom at the rear of the camper was closed and neither Valencia nor Nicole were anywhere in sight.

I mentioned my discovery to Valencia the next day.

"I couldn't help but notice something different in the camper," I said. "I must say, you're pretty a fast worker."

"You are very alert," he said. "I commend your power of observation."

"I don't mean to pry, but do you think it's wise?" I asked.

Valencia's handsome face had that look of ironic detachment that always came when he was amused by something.

"I don't know if it's wise, but I'm sure it's not stupid," he said. "And I don't think it effects what we're doing one way or the other."

I thought it over.

"You're right," I agreed. "It's none of my damn business."

The only interesting event over the next two days happened one night when Nicole had the watch-the-house detail and the rest of us followed the guys all day. By the time the long day was done, Tom, Dick, and Harry were all back in the house and it was one o'clock in the morning. There was no risk in Lilly, Valencia, and I linking up down the street behind a big tree with low-hanging branches that was on the same side of the street as the house. There were streetlights at each end of the block, but neither one worked. We could barely see Nicole down beyond the house on the other side of the street. She was standing outside the truck and stretching her legs, careful to keep the big Dodge between her and the house.

Two men came around the corner at Nicole's back, walking in that kind of sloppy way that told me they'd done more than their share of drinking. They snapped to attention when they saw an attractive woman hanging around on the sidewalk right in front of them, and their aggressive body language made their bad intentions clear as they moved in on Nicole, each one grabbing an elbow.

As far as they were concerned, the buffet was open.

Valencia and I started across the street, but Lilly grabbed my shoulder with one hand, extended her other arm in front of Valencia, and hissed, "Wait."

A thin shaft of moonlight broke through the clouds, illuminating the trio down the street as effectively as a spotlight.

Even from a distance, I heard the sharp metallic snap as Nicole's police baton telescoped opened. I never even saw it in her hand. Apparently her new friends didn't either. Worse than that, they didn't recognize the sound.

Nicole made a quick backhand motion and her victim cried out and doubled over, clutching his privates like he'd never let them go. Before the other one could react, Nicole pivoted to one side and brought the baton down across his kneecap. With a loud "Arrgh!" he went down like he'd been shot.

Nicole bent over and it looked like she was saying something, although she was too far away for us to hear it. I saw the baton rise and fall twice. She stood up, closed the baton on her hip, and slipped it back inside her belt.

Lilly stepped out into the street and waved one arm to get her attention. Nicole took a long look at the house to make sure the guys weren't disturbed by her little fracas. Satisfied that they weren't, she climbed into the truck and drove away, leaving her victims writhing on the sidewalk, one holding his knee while he rocked back and forth in pain, the other jackknifed and clutching himself.

"She would have hated it if we'd interfered," Lilly explained as she stoked up a cigarette. "Nikky doesn't like to be rescued."

Back at the trailer, before everybody turned in for the night I asked Nicole, "Did you stop and say something to your two friends there at the end, or was it just my imagination?"

"I explained to them that when a woman says, 'No,' chances are real good she means, 'No,'" she replied with an icy smile.

"You think they understood?" I asked. "Hell, they might not even speak English."

"I think I made my point," she said. "I gave 'em another couple of taps for emphasis."

"In that case, I'm sure they got it," I agreed.

CHAPTER 21

THE NEXT DAY we got the break we were waiting for.

After our usual three of us follow the guys, one of us watches the house routine, when we were sure they were through for the day we conducted our usual late-night post mortem at the picnic table outside the trailer. This being thirsty work, everybody had a Bohemia.

"I hit the mother lode today," Lilly announced.

"How's that?" I asked.

"Tom went to some big grocery store and bought about nine million pesos worth of groceries," she replied.

"Perhaps he was hungry," Valencia said wearily. "Everyone has to eat."

Lilly responded with a breathtaking smirk.

"Among other things, he bought Tampons."

Lilly, Nicole, and Valencia were grinning like this was better than Christmas. I realized that I was, too.

"Before we get too excited, let's stop and think this through," Valencia cautioned. "We have seen no girl-friends, mothers, or sisters anywhere, correct?'

"You don't buy Tampons for your mother or sister anyway," I said. "Maybe for your wife or girlfriend, but only maybe. It's been my experience that most women would rather do it themselves because they think it embarrasses men, or that a man might screw it up and buy the wrong kind, or something. He bought 'em because there wasn't any other choice. That means whoever he bought them for couldn't do it herself."

"And don't forget about all the groceries," Lilly added. "So far, these guys haven't struck me as domestic types. Tom bought enough to feed a lot of people."

"So let's say the groceries, at least most of them, are for somebody else?" Valencia mused. "Just like the Tampons."

"Like for Maria Tolsa and whoever's holding her, wherever that is," Nicole said.

"Was any of what Tom bought perishable?" I asked. "You know, fruit, vegetables, things like that?"

"Some," Lilly replied. I could tell that she saw where I was headed.

"So, assuming we're right, wherever they're taking it it'll have to be soon, before that stuff goes bad, and as hot as it is that probably isn't far," I said.

There were broad smiles all around as we reached into the center of the table and clinked our beer bottles.

"Tomorrow is going to be a good day," Valencia announced. "I can feel it already. I see no reason to change our pattern. It's best to continue according to schedule. Does everyone agree?"

Seeing assent, Valencia pushed back his chair, got to his feet, threw out his arms and stretched. It wasn't a very good performance.

"And now I think I'm ready for bed," he announced, which only added to the almost comic falsity of the scene.

With an exaggerated wave goodnight, he climbed up the steps into the trailer. A few seconds later, a light came on in the tiny bedroom.

After a long silence while Lilly and I waited for what

we knew was coming next, Nicole announced, "I guess I'll head inside, too."

She got to her feet and walked to the trailer, calling, "Night all" over her shoulder.

Lilly and I smiled at each other. I shrugged. Lilly rolled her eyes.

"I'm gonna take a walk," I said. "Wanna come?"

"Sure," she said.

I left my shoes underneath the table. Lilly did the same. We walked down to the beach, feeling the cool sand between our toes. We could see the faint glow of La Paz over the horizon. The ocean was so placid that the waves could have been measured in inches. The pungent smell of everything that has to do with the sea was all around us. I always loved that scent. There was something about it that spoke of adventure in far off lands, of pirates and broadsides and clashing swords and damsels in distress and extensive bodice ripping.

"As exits go, that one was about as awkward as I've ever seen," I said.

Even in the darkness I could see a grin play across Lilly's face. It made her look younger and less like a tough customer.

"There's never any graceful way, is there?" she agreed. "It was weird, though. It felt like we were a bunch of kids, or something."

We walked along the edge of the ocean, close enough so that the water edged up almost to our feet.

"How long have you two known each other?" I asked.

"Most of our lives. It seems funny when I say that, but it's true. We were ten or eleven when we met. We were best friends for a couple of years and then went our own ways the way kids do at that age. She discovered guys and popularity and the dean's list and I discovered ...."

Lilly hesitated, as if she was trying to find the right

words, or maybe she wasn't sure whether she should say anything at all.

"Not guys?" I suggested.

She laughed. It was a warm and relaxed laugh; even inviting, in its way. Except for singing Englebert Humperdinck's greatest hit on the drive north to La Paz, this was a side of Lilly that I hadn't seen.

"Yeah, something like that," she agreed. "We ran in different crowds in high school, a *lot* different. Anyway, by coincidence we had a class together our junior year in college and became friendly again. After graduation I went into the Army and Nicky went to work as an investigator for an insurance company. She got married a couple of years later. Years later, we hooked up again through a mutual friend. I was just out after re-enlisting twice. Nikky was single again and looking for something. Not just a job, but something that mattered, you know? Once we got to know each other all over again we realized that our experience dovetailed pretty well so we threw in together and started an agency. It was kind of slow at first. We're sort of an odd couple and sometimes people don't know what to make of us, but it usually works pretty well. Her strengths are my weaknesses and vice versa. Nikky's the best friend anybody could ever want, too. She's so loyal that she'll back you up even when you're wrong. But when it's over, she'll read you the riot act. Everybody looks at us and thinks I'm the tough one, but when it comes down to it, she's a lot tougher than I am."

"You said she was married. What happened to her husband?"

"He died in a car accident. Drunk driver. I didn't know her then, and I never met him, but everybody says they were the perfect couple; absolutely devoted to each other. They didn't have any kids. Nikky says they thought about adopting but never got around to it. Now she wishes they had. She thinks about it a lot. His death really wiped her out for a couple of years. I know it still bothers her sometimes. How could it not? That's why I'm glad to see her with Valencia. It's been a while since she's been with anybody. Nikky doesn't let her guard down much. Even if it doesn't mean anything in the long run, it'll be good for her."

We walked in silence. At this late hour, there was no one else on the beach. Even in the daytime, we'd only seen a couple of fishermen the whole time we'd been here. The sky was thick and glowing with thousands of stars. I was always struck by how many more stars I could see down here than I could on any night in the over-lit megalopolis of Southern California. In the far distance, I could see the lights from a couple of passing ships, probably cruise ships headed to Cabo, or maybe some kind of cargo ships going over to Mazatlan on the mainland across the Sea of Cortez. The tide was coming in so that even with the tiny waves the warm sea water swirled around our feet with every third or fourth wave.

"What about you?" Lilly asked. "How did you wind up living down here? I know Mexico's popular with American retirees, but you're a long way from retirement age."

For reasons I can't explain, I told her. Other than Dina and my shrink back in the states, I'd never told anyone the whole story of what happened to my parents and the kidnapping case gone wrong that put me in the hospital, not even Valencia.

When I finished, Lilly was quiet for a while.

"Your wife must be a hell of a lady," she finally said.

"She's all there is."

"If you don't mind my asking, how's it going now?"

"A lot better, most of the time," I replied. "Everything's fine for a while then something happens that brings it all back and it kind of overwhelms me. Sometimes I want to get out of this business, too. Actually a *lot* of the time I want to get out of this business and I even convince myself that I have. But then I never seem to actually *do* it. Something always happens."

"I've never wanted to get out, but I know how the rest of it feels," she said. "I've been through it with Nikky. I've had problems of my own, too. I guess everybody has. It's easy to forget that. I mean, everybody's got their own cross to bear. It's just that some crosses seem heavier than others, especially when it's yours."

I was tempted to ask what she meant about having problems of her own, but let it go. Enough secrets had been exchanged for one night. It was late, and it was time to go back and get some sleep. Big day tomorrow, at least we hoped so.

CHAPTER 22

I HAD Tom duty the next day. After loading so many boxes and sacks of groceries into the SUV that they were stacked almost to the roof, he left the house not long after noon. Lilly was right, there was enough food to feed half of La Paz.

As I rattled along behind Tom, it felt good to be moving after spending so many hours stewing on the street. There wasn't much traffic so I had to stay a long way back. After a few minutes, Tom turned onto the main highway headed south out of town. I continued to hang back, hoping like hell that he didn't have a lead foot. I doubted that the jeep could go faster than sixty five, if that. If Tom took off on me I was finished. All I'd be able to do is wave goodbye.

Fortunately, he didn't drive like a type A personality so I never had to test the jeep's maximum speed. Fifteen minutes out of La Paz, Tom left the highway to the right, taking a two-lane road headed more or less southwest. Traffic was still light. In fact, there wasn't any other traffic at all, which made the tail even trickier. It's a lot easier to do a tail if there's a little traffic to hide in. Fortunately, the road undulated so that I could hang back and still see the

SUV every time it topped a hill. When it went down the other side it disappeared until it reappeared at the top of the next hill. Even if he saw me, the pile of junk I was driving didn't exactly radiate danger.

After twelve minutes, the SUV raised a cloud of dust to the right as it left the road. When I got to the place where it turned, I was greeted by one of those uniquely Mexican sights - an ornate entrance to a development or resort that doesn't exist. It's a common sight in Mexico, at least in southern Baja. What usually happens is that the developer goes bust before he really gets started, leaving behind a fabulous entrance that leads to absolutely nothing. Like the façade on a movie set, a first impression is all there is. There were several such places scattered around Cabo San Lucas, each one representing a dream that was never to be.

I wasn't surprised when the smooth asphalt road came to an end just past the tall arched entrance with impressive Roman columns on each side. The entrance was commodious enough to accommodate two lanes each way, with a box for the guard in between. From where the asphalt ended a curving dirt road disappeared over a hill about a hundred yards away, where I could see the remains of the dust cloud raised by Tom's SUV. I got out of the jeep and took a good look at the SUV's tire tracks. In case I got too far behind, I wanted to make sure I'd recognize them if I saw them again. There were quite a few other tracks, too. Interesting.

I drove slowly so that I wouldn't raise a dust cloud of my own. When I got close to the top of the hill, I got my binoculars out of the glove compartment, walked to the top, and watched the SUV in the distance. It topped another hill and disappeared down the other side. I got back in the jeep and followed, driving even slower than before. When I neared the top of the hill where I last saw the SUV, I pulled off the dirt road into a small stand of scrub brush and got out. I don't know why, but I had the feeling that I was getting close to something. I felt some kind of presence looming the other side of the hill. Even if it turned out to be as empty as a cow pasture, I had nothing to lose by being careful.

I trudged to the top of the hill, binoculars in hand. It turned out that I didn't need the binoculars. Even though I halfway expected something to be there, I was so surprised that I had to remind myself to get down on my stomach before somebody spotted me standing there like I was waiting for the bus.

Spread out below was a sprawling collection of partially finished concrete-block buildings that were originally supposed to make somebody a fortune when they were made nice and built out, but now it was just another monument to what can happen when there's more ambition than money. Here and there naked rebar poked out of the unfinished concrete and pointed to the sky like the fingers of a skeleton.

There probably were a dozen buildings altogether. Several were two floors, with the top floors incomplete. The complex gave off an odd feeling. Instead of seeming unfinished - something that never existed as it was originally intended - it resembled a ruin, something that used to be but no longer was. The windows and doors were empty gaping holes and the walls were riddled with cracks. Five of the buildings ringed a large inner plaza, with a dry, weed-choked fountain in the middle. The resort that never was hadn't been landscaped before it was abandoned, so it was surrounded by dirt, scrub, and cactus as far as I could see. Some kind of awful music blared from inside one of the buildings.

Looking closer, I realized that one building was more finished than the others, a long two-story structure that ran across the top of the plaza. Like the other buildings, it had no installed windows or doors. But, unlike the others, the roof was complete, done in red tile, and the walls had been sprayed with stucco. Tom's SUV was parked beside the fountain and two men were unloading the groceries and carrying them into the building. Neither one of them was Tom.

I couldn't stay where I was and I didn't see a good place to hide the jeep. I was vulnerable if someone left and I was vulnerable if someone drove up. I scampered back to the jeep and carefully drove back the way I came, past the columned entrance to the two-lane road. After slowly driving a quarter of a mile back toward La Paz, I found what I was looking for. The road was raised over the rest of the countryside. One spot at the right where the road curved to the left was deep enough that if I parked the jeep below the road it couldn't be seen. I carefully bumped my way down and turned off the engine. The hard-baked earth was pretty firm, which was good because I did not trust the jeep's four-wheel drive capability. If it was too steep to drive back up to the road the way I came down, I could always parallel the road until I found an easier place to gain access.

I got out of the jeep, taking with me my SIG P210, my cell phone, the binoculars, the camera, a notebook and a couple of pencils. I climbed up to the road, confirmed that the jeep couldn't be seen from any direction, and started walking back the way I came. If somebody came up from either way, I'd hear it and have time to hide.

After forty minutes, I was soaked with sweat, but right where I wanted to be, in a tight stand of cactus about twenty five yards to the right of where I first spotted the unfinished complex. It was reasonably comfortable considering that I was lying on dirt in the middle of a cactus patch on a steaming Mexican day.

There was even a little shade. More important, it was fairly well hidden and offered a view of the complex. It wasn't perfect, but it would do.

After an hour, I'd seen six people, all of them men. Two of them carried hand guns. I counted eight vehicles parked around the place, five of them in the plaza. Figuring an average of one and a half people per car, that made twelve. Maybe there were more, and maybe there were less, but at least I had a baseline. It might not mean anything tomorrow if we found out more information, but it was all I had to work with today.

I saw a new man come out of the main building. As I did with everyone else, I took a good look through the binoculars. He wore a John Deere cap, khaki cargo pants with big pockets on the thighs, desert boots, and a long-sleeved denim shirt with the sleeves rolled up past his elbows. He had a weapon on his hip, but I couldn't tell what it was because it was hidden by the flap on his old-fashioned military holster. From what I could see under the cap, his scruffy black beard had a touch of premature gray in it. He was taller than a typical Mexican and filled out more, with broad shoulders and long legs. Maybe that was his Irish blood. Even with the binoculars, it was hard to tell with the cap shielding his face, but from the description we had I was pretty sure that I was looking at the elusive Bernardo O'Reilly.

He said something to a couple of men who were working on the engine of an old pick-up truck. O'Reilly, if that's who he was, slapped one man on the shoulder, everybody had a good laugh, and he went back inside the main building. There was a sense of authority in his manner with the men that told me he was the leader.

I called Valencia on my cell phone.

"*Hola*," he answered.

"I think I found O'Reilly," I whispered.

"Where are you?"

Keeping my voice to a whisper, I told him everything. The odometer on the jeep was broken, so I could only give an approximation of the distance, although I had pretty accurate numbers about driving speed and time.

"I'm coming out," he said.

"I don't think that's a good idea," I said. "This place is pretty isolated and there's no good way in that I can see, especially in the daylight. I was lucky I wasn't spotted when I got here. Why don't I stay here by myself until I put them to bed? I'll take some pictures and try to tally up how many people are here. Assuming she's here, I'll try to figure out where they might be holding Maria Tolsa, too."

There was silence on the other end. I knew that Valencia badly wanted to come. In his place, I would have. But that didn't mean it was the right thing to do. We were getting closer. This was no time to become impatient and blow it.

"All right," he said. "I'll see you tonight."

"I don't know when. It could be pretty late."

"We're not going anywhere," he said. "Call me if there are any changes or you need help."

I SPENT the rest of the hot day and several hours of the warm night lying on my belly while I watched, took pictures, made some really bad drawings of the compound and surrounding countryside, and was chewed on by a variety of vermin. Although I was badly tempted, I didn't leave my hiding place. I was pretty well hidden where I was. This was no time to tempt fate.

By midnight I was starving, tired as hell, and practically incontinent. Somebody down there was still awake because a light was on in one of the buildings and every so often somebody came out to do a half-hearted patrol. Since the complex probably wasn't wired for electricity, and I didn't hear a generator, I concluded that they must have gas or battery lamps. As best I could tell, they didn't have any other lookouts, although for safety's sake I had to assume that they did, even if I couldn't see them. If they didn't, they were pretty damn sloppy, but then we probably weren't dealing with Professor Moriarity and his vast criminal empire.

It was time to go, at last.

I slithered backwards out of the cactus patch, every muscle and joint in my body screaming in protest. I didn't get to my feet until I was most of the way down the hill. I was surprised by how much it hurt. If anything, walking was even more painful than crawling. It was a few minutes before I could do anything but awkwardly shuffle forward like I didn't have full control of my limbs.

By the time I got to the highway I was moving more or less naturally, although the walk to the jeep was a lot longer than I remembered. In the darkness every place looked the same as every other place, and it took a few minutes of blundering around before I found where I'd parked. I climbed into the jeep, which drew new and painful protests from an entirely different set of muscles, and slowly drove away without turning the lights on, looking for a good place to climb back up to the road. Once I did, I didn't speed up or turn the lights on until I was a couple of miles away. After that I couldn't go fast enough.

I was wrong about the jeep's top end. It didn't make it to sixty five. Sixty was all it had.

CHAPTER 23

When I got back to camp, I drank two beers in about eighteen seconds, ate two sandwiches made from some unrecognizable meat and wilted lettuce, and took a desperately needed shower.

Once I finished I was ready to display my digital photos and bad sketches and explain what I'd seen while Valencia, Lilly and Nicole listened with rapt attention.

When I ended my tale, Valencia said, "I know that place, or I should say that I know of it."

"Really?" I asked, peeling the tab off another beer. "How's that?"

"About ten years ago, with much fanfare, someone announced a plan to build a golf resort out there, along with a typical mix of condos and time shares," he explained. "But the developers, a *grupo* out of Guadala-jara, were undercapitalized. It did not help that the economy softened at that time. There were many delays, probably no more than usual with such an ambitious undertaking, but enough so that they were unable to finish what they started and lost their investment. All of it."

"What happened then?" Lilly asked.

"As far as I know, nothing," Valencia answered. "Whatever was built before the developers went out of business is all that's there. No one attempted to come in and complete what they started. It is not on the beach or close to it and it is thought to be too far away from La Paz for convenience."

"We need to know more about this place," Nicole said. "A lot more."

"We will," Valencia promised. "I will take care of it tomorrow. By the way, I talked to *Senor* Tolsa today. There is still no word from the kidnappers."

The fact that there hadn't been any word didn't mean that things were well with Maria Tolsa. While it didn't mean they were worse either, we all felt a sense of urgency. The longer this thing dragged out, the more likely it was that she would be hurt or killed.

After a night's sleep on the beach that was deep but not nearly long enough, I returned to the complex the next day and watched some more. This time I was prepared with food and water and slathered with insect repellent. Every time I saw a new face, I made an entry in my notebook, along with a brief description. A few more men came and went throughout the day while the awful music never stopped blaring some kind of Mexican rap. My favorite. I ended my count with a total of fifteen men, half of them armed. I assumed that the unarmed guys had weapons they weren't wearing when I saw them. I spotted five automatic weapons, too; AK 47s casually leaning in a row against the wall next to the door of the main building. A lot of firepower.

It was particularly interesting to see that two of the men were La Paz police in full uniform, a complication that we didn't need at all. There were no women, at least none that I saw. So either there really were no women - which made it hard to explain the Tampons - or what women there might be either kept out of sight or were forced to keep out of sight.

Everything pointed to this being the place. What were these people doing out here if not hiding? O'Reilly's presence – and it had to be O'Reilly; there's not that much coincidence in the world - certainly increased the chances that this was the gang that kidnapped Maria Tolsa. If she was there, I figured that she had to be in the central two-story building. For one thing, it was the most secure. For another, that's where O'Reilly seemed to be staying. The leader of the kidnappers would want the victim kept nearby, especially if we were right and some kind of obsession was involved.

Late in the morning, the day perked up when two men who were squatting on their haunches by the fountain playing some kind of dice game got into an argument. As I watched through the binoculars, the smaller one pulled a knife, making quick little flicking motions with it as they circled each other. Jerked out of their torpor, the rest of the gang gathered around to watch the action. Judging from what I'd see so far, it was the high point of their week.

Apparently hearing the commotion, O'Reilly charged out of the main building like a rabid wolverine. When he got between the combatants and shoved the little guy with the knife away, the bigger man saw his chance and charged. Without turning to face the charge, O'Reilly raised one bent arm and rapped the big guy on the beezer with the point of his elbow. Seeing his foe stagger back with one hand clutching at his face, the smaller man moved in with his knife low, ready to gut the opposition. But O'Reilly was quicker, a lot quicker. He caught the knife hand at the wrist, turned into the little guy, caught his weight on his shoulders and flipped him into the air so that he landed on his back with a thump that even I could hear, the wind and the fight knocked out of him.

O'Reilly bent down, picked up the knife and put it in his belt. He helped the man who'd taken the shot to the nose to his feet, then did the same for the little guy, who still was laboring to get his wind back. Standing between them, he put an arm around the shoulders of each man and walked them in a tight little circle, talking all the time. After a minute or two, there was sort of a group hug while everybody patted everybody else on the back with apologies all around. Peace made, O'Reilly went back into the building, the knife still in his belt.

I was impressed. O'Reilly knew his stuff. He'd broken up a fight before it got serious, put two men down without really hurting either one of them, and then made them love him for it. They did everything but sit around the campfire and sing "Kumbaya."

Three hours later, as the afternoon edged into the traditional *siesta* time in Mexico and everybody was at their least energetic in the oppressive heat, I took a chance and explored the terrain by making a wide circle around the complex. Careful not to show myself, or leave any sign that I'd passed, it took more than two hours of painstaking labor and sweat to make the full circle.

While the road from the highway was the only road in, the place could be approached from any direction by walking in, riding horses, or with a four-wheel drive vehicle, although the noise would make the latter difficult to conceal. It would be better to leave it a safe distance away and walk the rest of the way. A vehicle would be good to have if we had to make a fast getaway, too. The problem was that if we left it a safe distance away, we'd be on foot until we got to it.

I had no idea how far it was to civilization in any

direction other than the way I came in. I assumed that was one of the things Valencia was finding out. For the second day in a row, I saw no lookouts other than one guy doing a sloppy patrol. For one thing, he was too regular. He had a pattern and never deviated from it. Whatever they thought of themselves, with the exception of O'Reilly this was a bunch of amateurs, unless they were so good that they fooled me into thinking they were amateurs. But if they didn't know I was here, why would they do that? I decided that I'd been out in the sun too long. I was starting to chase my own tail. Besides, amateurs can be more dangerous than pros because you never know what they'll do.

After my patrol, I settled in and watched some more. Shortly after before 2 a.m., with everybody but the patrol inside nothing more for me to see, I called it a night.

Back at camp, Valencia produced the property records and a detailed map of the area, plus the blue prints of the buildings as they were supposed to have been built before the developer crashed. The records confirmed what he told us the night before.

As we sat around the picnic table and poured over the maps by the artificial light of the gas lamp, Nicole asked, "Why don't you give us the short version for now. We can do the details later. Just how accessible is this place?"

"Difficult but doable," Valencia explained. "As Ethan said, if you approach on the road from La Paz you will be visible because there's no place to hide. Even if no one is watching, you can be seen at any time by anyone who happens to be coming or going. Like Ethan, I find it hard to believe that they don't have lookouts except for one man, but if they're that careless then it's our good luck. The best approach would be from the rear. It is, needless to say, desert, so there is not much cover except for cactus, rocks, and brush."

Using the point of a knife, Valencia pointed to a thin curving line on the map that ran up close to the site. "However, there *is* a dry river bed that we may be able to use." He nodded at me. "I doubt that it can be seen from the complex. It may turn out to be of no help, but it's a possibility to be checked out. However we go in we must take advantage of whatever cover there is, and if they're not looking, and if we're a lucky …."

"*If*, brother, *if*," I said.

Valencia sat back in his chair and ran his fingers through his dark hair. He looked tired in the flickering light. We all did.

"I know, but unless there's an unexpected change in the situation I don't see another way," he said. "We can't wait forever and they seem very well set up. It's obvious they're not impatient or they would have contacted Tolsa by now."

"Assuming Mrs. Tolsa *is* there, getting into this place won't be easy, but getting her out will be damned difficult," Lilly said. "We haven't even talked about that yet."

"Yes, it will be hard," admitted Valencia. "And dangerous, too."

"And we can't go to the La Paz cops because from what Ethan saw they're involved in this," Nicole added. "We don't know if it's just the cops he saw, or the whole department's dirty."

We sat there and stared at the map, each of us with our own thoughts. I suspected that none of them were happy thoughts either.

"If anyone wants to leave, now is the time to say so," Valencia said. "This may turn into something more than we thought. It already has, I suppose. There is no blame attached to anyone who drops out. That may be the wisest move."

Lilly was the first to break the silence.

"As that great philosopher W. C. Fields once said, there comes a time when you have to seize the bull by the tail and face the situation."

Nicole translated.

"She means we're staying,"

CHAPTER 24

LILLY HAD a pilot's license that was valid in Mexico so we decided to take a look at the complex and surrounding countryside from the air. I knew from hard experience that doing it that way instead of on the ground would save a lot of time and labor.

After assessing the small selection of aircraft available for hire at the La Paz airport, we rented a Cessna Skyhawk. Once the little single-engine four-seater was checked out and loaded with fuel, we took off from a dirt runway that private planes used, not from the big international airport next door. Not being fond of heights, I had my usual nervousness in a small plane. But Lilly was so obviously competent at the controls that I quickly relaxed, as least as much as I was ever going to. Lilly and I sat in the front, with Nicole and Valencia in the rear seats. Nicole, Valencia and I had binoculars and Nicole brought her camera with a telephoto lens. The Skyhawk's wings were above the cabin so we had an unobstructed view of the ground.

Once she had the Skyhawk leveled off, Lilly asked, "White knuckle flier?" She had to shout to be heard over the Cessna's engine.

"Don't take it personally," I said. "It's more of a height problem than a flying problem. It doesn't bother me in commercial jets. I didn't know it was so obvious."

"You're being careful to look out and not down," she said with a grin. "That's always a giveaway."

"I'll try to remember that," I said. "Just don't bank hard to the right or you'll see what I had for breakfast."

I laughed to show that I was just joking; at least I hoped I was just joking.

For a distraction, I twisted to my left so I could see Valencia and Nicole.

"Won't they get suspicious on the ground if we make several passes?"

"I don't think so," Valencia replied. "We'll only make two passes at most. The site is close enough to the airport so that aircraft probably fly over quite often. Besides, we're more interested in the surrounding country than we are in the site itself. You've already seen everything there is to see there."

We'd leveled off for only a few minutes when Lilly shouted, "We'll be coming up on it pretty soon, off to the right."

A couple of minutes later, we spotted it. Lilly gently banked to the right. She patted my arm reassuringly when I gave her a thumbs up by way of thanks. From the air, the complex looked like a collection of one-dimensional rectangles positioned in a precise pattern that wasn't obvious from ground level. The buildings were equidistant from each other and set meticulously around the plaza with the dry fountain. As I'd seen from the ground, only the main two-story building had a finished roof, with the red tile that was so popular in Mexico and all over the American southwest.

On our second pass, using my binoculars I saw a

temporary palapa roof inside the one-story building that was closest to the main building. It was probably built to protect whoever was staying in the building from the sun more than from what little rain fell here. It was below the roof line, which explained why I hadn't seen it from the ground. That meant that at least two of the buildings probably were occupied, which also confirmed what I'd seen from ground level.

Nicole leaned forward and shouted into my ear.

"Just like you described it. Good job."

After two passes that gave Nicole a chance to use her long-lens camera to get some detailed shots, we turned our attention elsewhere.

The dry river bed ran toward the complex at an angle, roughly from southeast to northwest. The ancient river cut a winding channel several feet below the surrounding countryside. From the air it looked like it was impassable, choked with brush and weeds, although it probably wasn't that bad on the ground. At its closest point, the channel was about three hundred yards from the southwest corner of the complex. If we followed the river bed to get as close as we could, it might effectively conceal us until we had to leave it to cover the ground between it and the complex.

After flying several widening circles, we didn't see any other approach that looked as promising, so we turned back to the river bed. Going one way it ended at the coast, maybe ten miles south of La Paz, where once upon a time the river flowed into the Sea of Cortez. Going the other way, it turned north into the spine of the Baja Peninsula. If we used the river bed as a way in and out, starting on the coast was the route to use. The other way didn't take us anywhere we wanted to go.

An hour after we took off, Lilly smoothly landed the

Skyhawk back at the airport. My stomach lurched, but only mildly

"See, you lived through another one," Lilly joked.

"I never doubted it for a minute," I said.

It looked like we'd found a way in. Now it would be nice to come up with a way out.

CHAPTER 25

"Is THERE a possibility that any of you know how to use this little item?"

Valencia had just driven into camp after spending most of the day in La Paz. He got out of the jeep and walked to the table, carrying a grenade launcher over his shoulder.

"Where in the hell did you get that?" Lilly asked.

"I know some people," Valencia replied. "I had a feeling they might be able to come up with something like this, for a substantial fee, of course."

"Just what do they do that they have access to that thing, much less sell it?" I asked.

"Their business is always changing." Valencia smiled, revealing his brilliantly white teeth. "They like to keep things fluid. Some days it's one thing; some days it's another. They are very entrepreneurial."

Nicole had a good laugh at that. Always an attractive woman, now she seemed to positively glow. She and Valencia had stopped trying to pretend they weren't lovers. Their relationship had become very touchy feely and full of long significant looks. It was a side of Valencia that I hadn't seen before. It was as if they both knew that what they had wouldn't last very long so they decided to make it count all they could.

"I swear to God, if we needed a full dress uniform to outfit an admiral in the Turkish navy, you'd wander off somewhere and come back with one all cleaned, pressed, and ready to go," Nicole said.

"Probably from one of your 'cousins,'" I added.

Valencia laid the weapon on the picnic table. He walked back to the jeep, lifted a wooden box out of the back seat, carried it to the table on his shoulder, and laid it on the ground.

Nicole motioned in Lilly's direction.

"To answer your original question, she knows how to use it."

"At least I did a long time ago," Lilly added. "I haven't touched one in years. Not since the army."

"Don't worry," I said. "It's like riding a bicycle."

"Oh good," she said. "That makes me feel *so* much better."

"As you already know, this is a Soviet-era RPG-7 anti-tank grenade launcher," Valencia explained. "It's shoulder launched, muzzle loaded, and extremely portable at only fifteen pounds. It has a maximum effective range of three hundred meters against moving targets and five hundred meters against stationary targets. The true practical range is more like one hundred and fifty to two hundred meters, depending on the target. All you need is a clear view and an unimpeded pathway where the grenade can fly without being deflected by foliage. It was quite a deadly piece of equipment in Afghanistan, Somalia, and Iraq, among other places, especially against armored vehicles and helicopters."

"I seem to remember a downside to these things, too," Lilly said. "Once you fire it, you better haul ass because you're awfully easy to spot."

"The launch signature is unmistakable - a bright flash and a cloud of whitish blue-gray smoke," Valencia admitted. "But you'll be shooting at night, so the smoke should not be as much of a factor. As for the flash, if everything works as we hope it will, you should be finished and away before anybody figures out where you are."

"Ammo?" asked Nicole.

Valencia pointed to the box.

"Six rounds. I'm afraid that is all I could get on short notice."

"And what, exactly, are we supposed to shoot at?" Lilly asked. "Would you mind filling us in on a few things ... like, for instance, the details?"

Lying on our bellies in my cactus patch and then slithering around to the dry river bed to make sure that it offered the cover we thought it did when we saw it from the air, Valencia and I had worked out a plan. We agreed that while it just might be possible to pull it off, but we needed an equalizer, something that would increase our chances of success. Valencia thought he knew where he might be able to find it and left early in the morning.

We spread the most-detailed of our maps on the table and explained what we'd come up with. Lilly and Nicole made a comment here and a suggestion there, all of them good. It didn't take long for everything to come together.

Approaching the site shouldn't be a problem, although we'd have to be careful. The problem was getting into the complex, finding Maria Tolsa, and getting away. By now, we were certain that she was held in the main two-story building. There didn't seem to be any other possibility. Under the cover of darkness, Valencia and I were confident that we could get in all right. Either we'd find her pretty quickly or we were wrong about everything and she wouldn't be there at all. But to get away we needed a diversion to guarantee a head start and a way to slow down the pursuit and reduce the numbers. We hoped that the grenade launcher would do all three; distract, delay, and reduce.

"They bunch their transportation in the plaza, so it'll make a nice fat target for this baby," I said, fondly patting the grenade launcher like I was patting Brewster on the head. "It's designed for use against light armor, so cars, trucks, and SUVs shouldn't be much of a problem."

"We'll have to time it exactly, so that we find the Tolsa woman and are on our way out before you start shooting," Valencia said. "Ethan's cactus patch looks like your best position. It offers the best combination of cover, location, and unimpeded line of fire. Park your truck by the side of the road in the same spot where we parked the jeep and walk in, being careful to avoid the road. That way they won't hear the diesel. We'll come in through the dry river bed. We'll get as close as we safely can, then walk the rest. A half or three-quarters of a mile should do it."

"The thing is, they won't know you're shooting only at the vehicles," I added. "They'll think somebody big is moving in on them; maybe federal or army. If anybody's inclined to harm the hostage, we'll have her by the time you start shooting. As soon as you think you've done all the damage you reasonably can, get the hell out even if you haven't used all the grenades. In fact, it's probably a good idea to save something in case you're pursued."

"What then?" Nicole asked.

"If no one's after you, come back here," I said. "But make sure you're not followed. If someone *is* after you, lose them, outrun 'em, or put 'em out of business with the grenade launcher."

"What about you two?" asked Lilly.

"We'll go back the way we came, following the river bed toward the coast, hopefully taking Maria Tolsa with us," Valencia answered. "If they're not chasing us, or at least if they're not too close, we'll come back here, too."

"And if they are chasing you?" she asked.

""Same as you, we lose 'em, outrun 'em, or find a way to put 'em out of action," I said. "But no matter what happens, *this* is the rendezvous. We're not to link up until we're all back here. We can't try to help each other. In the dark, it's too hard to tell the good guys from the bad guys. If you know we're not around, and we know you're not around, that makes everybody we run into a bad guy."

"Why not communicate by cell phone instead of going by the clock?" Lilly asked. "Tell us when you find her, *if* you find her, then we start shooting."

"We thought of that, but we don't know about cell phone reception down there in the buildings, or even around them," I said. "It was okay at the cactus patch but we don't know about anywhere else. It's best not to rely on the phones, especially out in the boondocks. They're too iffy. We're going to do this the old fashioned way."

The sense of anticipation was so strong that it was like another presence at the table. The tension was building already.

"Okay, when do we go in?" Nicole asked.

"Tomorrow night," replied Valencia. "At eleven."

Nicole frowned as she used her fingers to rake her hair out of her eyes. I had a pretty good idea what she was going to say because Valencia and I had already talked about it.

"From what Ethan said, at least some of 'em are still up and around then," she said. "Why not wait until they're asleep? Say at two or three in the morning, or something?"

"Because somebody's awake all the time, even if they're pretty sloppy about keeping watch," I replied.

"There's always somebody patrolling. If we wait until everybody's asleep, we'll never go."

"But more that that, you must remember that darkness is our friend," Valencia added. "It's a long way back here. It will take time. We'll want to use all the darkness we can, especially if they're after us. It would not be a good thing for any of us to be outnumbered and trapped in the daylight. We don't want to go in too early, but we don't want to go in too late either."

The argument won Nicole over. That was it. Almost. There was only one more thing I wanted to say.

"Please remember what we're here for."

I stood up so I could look down at the rest of them gathered around the redwood table.

"There's a young woman out there who's scared to death. She was ripped away from her home and saw at least one man murdered in the process, probably more. Even if they haven't harmed her, that doesn't mean they won't and she knows it. She may not even know where she is or who kidnapped her. None of us can imagine what Maria Tolsa's going through. If we're lucky, that's something we'll never have to know. Getting her away from those people is what we're here for. Nothing else matters. Let's remember that."

"Thank you, Knute Rockne," Lilly said.

"Yeah," I said, "I'm sure the Gipper would want it this way.

CHAPTER 26

I CALLED Dina the next day.

Although I knew that my shrink would chastise me for it, I didn't intend to tell her what we were about to do. She would only worry herself silly and it wouldn't help anything.

I could hear him scold me now. He'd probably even wag his finger. I'd seen that a lot.

"She's earned the right to worry about you," he'd say. "Either she's in your life or she's not. Either she's your companion or she isn't. Not saying anything insults and diminishes her. If it was turned around, how would you feel? It's also a bad sign. It means that you're falling back on your old habits of repression, and we know where that can lead, don't we?"

Yes, doctor, we know where that can lead; right back into the booby hatch. And while we're at it why don't you go piss up a rope? It all seems pretty easy when it's not you, doesn't it? Jerk.

Even as I listened to this irritating inner dialogue, I knew that he was right, which was pretty strange considering that he hadn't actually said anything. But it still was a lot easier to say nothing to Dina about what we were going to do. I justified it by telling myself that right now I didn't need something else on my mind. If that made me a selfish bastard, well, I could live with it. I was a selfish bastard no matter what I did. Welcome to my world.

"How's it going up there?" she asked.

The cell phone reception was lousy. She sounded like she was talking into a bucket.

"Pretty boring," I lied. "We do a lot of watching and sweating in parked cars."

At least that part was true. Nobody *lies* all the time.

"How are things there?" I asked.

"Pretty good, except you're not here. I landed another account, a big one, too. Brewster misses his daddy. He keeps looking out the window, waiting for you to come home. If I wasn't so grownup, I'd probably do the same thing."

I was homesick, too. I was also a lying selfish bastard, although I told myself that good intentions count for something. Unfortunately I knew better. I didn't want to worry Dina unnecessarily, except that I was about to do something that might be pretty dangerous, so the worry probably wasn't unnecessary. What I really didn't want is to start worrying about her worrying about me. So that meant I was lying for my benefit, not for hers. I'm a rotten lying selfish bastard, no doubt about it.

"Got any idea of how much longer you'll be there?" she asked.

"Not really," I said. "We have some possibilities, but nothing sure yet."

"How are Nicole and Lilly doing?"

"Great," I said. "They're real pros. It's a pleasure to work with them. Oh, yeah, Nicole and Valencia are an item now."

"An *item*?" She giggled. "When did my husband morph into Hedda Hopper?"

"Okay, allow me rephrase it," I said. "They're screwing like bunnies. You dated yourself with the Hedda Hopper reference, by the way. You must be really old."

"It's all the history I read," she said. "Any more contact from the kidnappers? A note, or a call, or a message in a bottle? Anything at all?"

I was on less swampy ground now. At least I could tell the truth.

"Not a word. Valencia checks every day, even though that's really not necessary. Tolsa would let us know right away if he heard anything."

"Isn't that kind of strange? I mean, it's been a while. Shouldn't you have heard something more by now?"

"Maybe, but I really don't know. Not down here anyway. There's no such thing as a normal kidnapping, I guess. There's no rulebook to follow."

Keep babbling Cruickshank. Hide the fact that you're deceiving the love of your life with a tremendous fog of blather. You're actually pretty good at this, aren't you? Rotten lying selfish bastard.

"I guess I better go," I said.

"Okay. You be careful. Say 'hi' to Valencia for me. And tell him not to exhaust himself in the throes of passion. I need him to watch out for you."

"I will, though I probably won't use those exact words, the 'throes of passion' part."

"I love you."

"I love you, too."

Why shouldn't I be a rotten lying selfish bastard? I've had a lifetime of practice.

Except that a guilty conscience got the better of me. Who knew? For every minute that passed after we talked, the worse I felt. Knowing that I deserved it just made the load heavier. After an hour, I couldn't stand it anymore and called Dina again.

"Hi, kid," I said.

"What a nice surprise," she said. "A twofer."

"Maybe. You see, the thing is I didn't quite tell you everything the first time."

"So you called back to tell me the parts you forgot or something?"

"Kind of … not really. I didn't want to worry you. It's dumb, I know. But … I'm …."

"Ethan, why don't you just come out say it? Open your mouth, try not to over think it, and let the words come out. Even if you mess it up, at least it's a start and we can go from there."

The words came in a rush, as if I wanted to say them all along.

"We're pretty sure they're holding Maria Tolsa. It's an unfinished development outside of La Paz. We're going in to grab her. Nicole and Lilly will create a diversion while Valencia and I do the grabbing. It might be easy. It might be hard. There's no way to tell. But I didn't say anything before because I didn't want you to worry. I know that's wrong, but … I …."

"Ethan, it's okay. It's really okay."

I expected anger and didn't get it. Her voice was calm and understanding and it made me feel better. I'd underestimated her. Again.

"The thing is, you told me. I know it was a hard thing to do and it goes against the way you are, but you told me. So the next time maybe you'll be able to do it on the first try. It's okay."

"Really?"

"Really," she said.

CHAPTER 27

I DREAMED AGAIN THAT NIGHT.

I was chasing one of Maria Tolsa's kidnappers. I don't know how I knew he was one of them, but I did. I had my gun out, but it was dark and I couldn't see him clearly. We were on a beach, but it wasn't any beach that I knew, or one that seemed to exist anywhere in the world. It was hard plowing through the sand and the harder I worked at it, the slower I moved. I was sweating, my breath was labored, and the pounding of the surf was louder and louder.

Suddenly the kidnapper turned on me and everything changed. My heart jumped in my chest like a gaffed fish. Now I was in my parents' bedroom. My mother and father were in their bed. They were sitting up against the headboard with pillows at their backs. Two men stood over them with baseball bats on their shoulders. It was the same old picture, and yet it was different. My parents were screaming and I couldn't hear them. I couldn't hear anything. But I knew that they were screaming and begging me to shoot the men.

I raised my gun and pulled the trigger but nothing

happened. I tried it again and again. Still nothing. The two men didn't even notice me. It was like I was invisible. When they raised the bats over their heads, my mother looked at me for the last time in her life. She said something, but there was no sound, although I could hear her question inside my head while her eyes accused me.

"Why didn't you help us? Why?"

Something was clawing at my shoulder. I fought it off before I jerked awake with a start that left me confused. I was curled up on a cheap chaise lounge on the beach outside of La Paz, Mexico. In the torment of the dream, I'd thrown my blanket off and it was lying twisted on the sand next to my chair. Lilly was beside me. She was on her knees in the sand with one hand resting lightly on my bare shoulder.

"Ethan? Ethan? Wake up!"

I was disoriented inside and out. It was like I'd lost my place in the world and knew that I could never find it again.

"Are you okay?"

I blinked and rubbed my eyes, breathing hard.

"It was just a bad dream," I said. "I'm all right. Sorry if I woke you up."

Lilly gently patted me on the shoulder. My skin was clammy and her hand was comforting.

"You didn't. I couldn't sleep. I was laying there thinking about coming outside for a smoke when I heard you yell, except it was more like a scream, and I came running out. It looked like you were fighting something. You were shouting and writhing on the chair. I thought you were going to fall off."

She hesitated, then asked, "Are you sure you're okay?"

"I'm okay, really."

I was, too. I was fully conscious now. It was over, at least until the next time.

"Please don't tell me I woke up Nicole and Valencia, too?"

"I don't think so," she said.

Her mouth curled up at the edges; the beginning of a smile.

"They have the door closed, as usual. They probably screwed themselves to sleep."

Lilly was still on her knees in the sand beside my chaise lounge, with her weight resting on the back of her legs. She looked younger in the dark, more open and vulnerable, which was kind of strange considering that right now I was the vulnerable one.

"I don't mean to intrude, but would you like me to stay out here with you for a little while?" she asked. "I wouldn't mind. I wasn't sleeping anyway."

I couldn't see Lilly's face very well, but her voice was kind. I wanted her to stay, if only for a few minutes, but at the same time I didn't want to ask her. My pride and my need fought it out and my pride won. It always did.

"I'm okay now, I really am," I said. "It's over now. Why don't you try to get some sleep? Tomorrow's going to be a pretty tough day for everybody."

It was one of those rare moments when we both knew what the other was feeling despite the words that denied it. Lilly knew that I wanted her to stay but she was too tactful to say so. She took her hand off my shoulder, rose to her feet, and brushed the sand off her knees. I could feel her emotionally reaching out to me in the darkness. If I wanted her to stay, she seemed to be saying, it was okay to say so. Nobody's brave all the time. Instead of giving voice to it, she just stood there for a moment, giving me the chance to change my mind. I could see her outline and the glitter of her eyes, but everything else was darkness. When I remained silent she smiled and then headed back to the camper.

"Lilly," I said.

She turned around.

"Thank you."

"That's okay," she said. "I know how it is sometimes."

CHAPTER 28

VALENCIA and I rattled along the dry river bed in the old wreck of a jeep; zigzagging back and forth as we dodged clumps of scrub and rocks, many of them bigger than the jeep.

"Tell me one more time why we took this rust bucket instead of something that was built sometime in the last forty years," I shouted.

Valencia's gloved hands gripped the steering wheel in the ten and two o'clock positions. His eyes never left our path, or at least they wouldn't have left it if there actually was a path. Although we weren't going very fast, every so often we bottomed out with a teeth-rattling thump when the river bed laid a surprise on us.

"It may be old, but it's an excellent off-road vehicle and its coloring is as good as camouflage," he replied, shouting, like I did, to be heard above the engine's roar. "And if something happens to it …."

"It'll be just another abandoned wreck and no one will miss it, probably not even its owner," I shouted, finishing the thought for him. "I don't blame him either."

With more ground to cover, we left camp well ahead of Nicole and Lilly. It was a moment that cried out for some dramatic statement or gesture, but either nobody had one to make or nobody wanted to bother. We synchronized our watches and Valencia and I drove away. It was as simple as that. Over the years, I've found that one of the problems with thinking of yourself as a pro is that from time to time you have to act like one. Dramatic gestures are nice in movies, but they don't work as well in real life, where they just seem corny and forced. Unless you're Knute Rockne, I guess

I was wearing Wrangler jeans, black over-the-ankle Rockports, and a black long-sleeved pullover shirt. My SIG P210 was holstered on my hip and the Colt was in a shoulder holster outside my shirt. I felt like Wild Bill Hickok. Valencia was dressed in black and had his Glock on his hip. If nothing else, at least we were well armed and hard to see.

It was a clear and virtually cloudless night. The moon was just a sliver in the black sky and didn't give off much light, one of the reasons why we decided to go in when we did, although a few clouds over the moon would have been nice, too. In the darkness, the twisted shapes of the desert seemed eerie and unreal. It felt like we were moving across the surface of another planet.

The ride seemed interminable. It didn't help that I looked at my watch every five minutes. We were going by time as much as by distance. Finally Valencia stopped and made a careful three-point turn in the river bed so that the jeep faced the way we'd come. By our rough estimate, we were about three-quarters of a mile from the site, maybe a little less.

We covered the remaining ground at a walk; not too fast to be careless, but not too slow either. Three times I scrambled up the sloping side of the river bed to look over the rim and check our bearings. The third time we were within fifty yards of where we wanted to be; about three hundred yards away from the unfinished building that was closest to the river bed.

We weren't supposed to move in until ten minutes before Nicole and Lilly were scheduled to start shooting, so we had a forty minute wait, time we'd factored in if we were delayed on the way. It was better to be early than late. It was impossible to see very much from where we were. The plaza with the dry fountain was out of sight on the other side of the buildings. All we could do was wait in the darkness, and waiting is the hardest thing of all.

Valencia's night glasses were hanging from a leather strap around his neck and he raised them to peer toward the buildings.

"See anything?" I whispered.

"There's a door on this side of all three buildings closest to us," he said. "It would be very helpful if there was a similar door on this side of the main building, too. Then we … put your head down!"

I eased down the embankment so that my head was below the rim. Valencia did the same, only not all the way. His head was still slightly above the rim, just enough so that he could see through the glasses.

"It's the patrol. Just one man, as usual. He's come around to the back."

Valencia watched a little longer.

"How long did you say it took them to make the rounds? About ten minutes?"

"Almost exactly, every time," I replied. "It's one of their weaknesses."

"The next time he comes around I'm going to take him. They won't have a chance to miss him before Lilly and Nicole start the party."

"Need any help?"

Valencia lowered the goggles.

"It's better if there's just one of us," he whispered. "You can watch from here in case anyone else comes up. I wouldn't want any surprises."

As usual, somebody had a radio, or a stereo, or maybe an i-pod on, perhaps the same one I'd heard before. We could hear the sound of the music without being able to identify what kind of music it was. Considering what I heard when I watched the place earlier, I was glad that we couldn't hear it very well. Maybe it was their way of torturing their captive?

A couple of minutes before the one-man patrol was scheduled to reappear, Valencia handed over the night glasses and touched the thin blade he wore on his right hip to make sure that it was loose in its leather scabbard. Without a sound, he crawled over the rim and down the slight incline on the other side. After a few feet he disappeared into the darkness.

I lifted the glasses to my eyes. I could see him moving rapidly and precisely at a half-crouch. I scanned the buildings to make sure no one came out. Valencia stopped at a pile of rocks and brush that had been deposited there long ago when the river flooded and overflowed its banks, impossible as that seemed now. There were only about a half-dozen rocks, and none of them were taller than three feet, but when he got down low he couldn't be seen by anyone on the other side, although I could see him clearly from my position.

The patrol reappeared from around the corner of the building furthest away from Valencia. He leaned against the wall and lit a cigarette. I couldn't tell if he was armed, but every patrol that I'd seen had a weapon either on his hip or tucked into his waistband. I assumed this one was no different.

As I watched him on the last walk he'd ever take, he followed the same path as all the others; a long shallow curve around the back of the buildings. To do it right, he should have come all the way out to the river bed, but we already knew that security was pretty sloppy. At the outermost part of the curve his path was such that his back was to Valencia, who was waiting behind the rocks about thirty feet away.

With the knife in his right fist, Valencia pounced. He covered the ground so fast that even if the patrol heard him he didn't have time to turn and react. Through the glasses, I saw the thin blade strike horizontally at the small gap between the first vertebra and the base of the skull. When it's done right, there's little bleeding, no sound, and almost instant death. I knew these things only theoretically. I'd never killed anyone that way. Watching Valencia, it was clear that he knew from experience. Without letting his victim fall, Valencia clasped his arms through the dead man's armpits and dragged him back to his hiding place behind the rocks.

I scanned the buildings to make sure that no one had come out. After waiting behind the rocks for a moment, Valencia returned to our hiding place, moving as noiselessly as when he left. When he came up over the rim and flopped down beside me, even in the darkness I could see a glistening smudge on the thigh of his black jeans, where he'd wiped the blood off his knife.

"How long?" he asked, breathing as if he'd taken a brisk walk, but nothing more.

"Nine minutes."

It probably wasn't the longest nine minutes of my life, but it certainly felt like it. I kept waiting for something to go wrong: for someone to come around back and discover the body; for Lilly and Nicole to fire too soon; for someone to discover where they were hiding; for someone to discover where we were hiding; for someone to find the jeep; and for a dozen other things, all of them bad, but none of them happened.

Finally, it was time.

We went up and over the top, covering the ground as silently as we could. Although I moved well and quietly, I felt like a rhinoceros compared to Valencia, who flitted across the ground like a shadow. We didn't stop until we reached the building closest to us, where we flattened our backs against the wall and caught our breath. I nodded and Valencia moved toward one corner and I went toward the other.

I waited to see if I could hear any telltale sounds from the other side before I stuck my head out. There was nothing between me and the main building, which had a doorway on this side, just as we hoped. A light from somewhere inside the building cast a faint elongated glow through the gaping doorway. There was a light on the second floor, too, up and to the right of the doorway. It was probably the same light.

I returned to our original position, where Valencia was waiting.

"The door's right there," I whispered. "It couldn't be better if we ordered it. What about you?"

"Yours is best."

Back at my corner, Valencia stuck his head out, peered through the night glasses, pulled back and shook his head. The light from upstairs made it impossible to see anything with the glasses. Using the naked eye, he made sure everything was clear, and then motioned me forward. I drew the SIG. Staying light on my feet, I ran to the main building while Valencia covered me.

I flattened against the wall about ten feet from the doorway and motioned Valencia forward. He drew his Glock and made the same run, only to the other side of the doorway. Now that we were this close it was clear that the light shining through the doorway came from somewhere upstairs, which probably meant that there was nobody downstairs, unless they were asleep. The music was louder now; but not as loud as the thumping of my heart.

We waited as if time would give us a sense of what might be waiting for us through the doorway. And who knows, maybe it did? Without knowing how I knew, I was sure that the answer was nothing. Whoever was inside the building, and someone certainly was, they were upstairs.

We edged forward so that we were just outside of the doorway on either side. I nodded at Valencia. He went through at a crouch and flattened himself against the wall just inside so that I could see him. Once he was sure of the situation, he motioned me in, where I joined him against the wall.

As I suspected, there was no one inside, although there were many signs of life, if you want to call it that. Blankets, pillows, and sleeping bags were carelessly scattered across the bare cement floor, while a collection of fast-food containers, beer and soft-drink cans and bottles, some clothing, and a variety of other human detritus littered the area.

I motioned toward a bare, unfinished cement stairway on the other side of the room. Moving soundlessly, Valencia crossed the open space and took a position beneath it. He peered up the stairs to make sure no one was waiting at the top and motioned me forward. Even with the thin light, after being so long in darkness I felt naked and vulnerable as I crossed the room. We waited for another moment to make sure we hadn't been heard and then started up the stairs, Valencia taking the lead.

The light came from a room all the way down the hall at the top of the stairs. We moved in on opposite sides of the hall. Ropes of beads hung from the top of the doorway to give the doorless room the illusion of privacy. After pausing in the shadows of the hall, and making sure to keep outside of the light, we edged closer to the doorway, one of us on each side.

The beads made it easy to see inside. Maria Tolsa, darkly beautiful and surprisingly healthy looking, sat on a rough wooden bench at a small table. She was looking into a cracked mirror hanging on the wall while she combed her long black lustrous hair. The room was sparsely furnished, with only the table, the bench, the mirror, a gas lamp on the table, and a narrow bed.

A tall muscular man came through the doorway on the wall at a right angle from us. He was dressed in jeans, a white pullover shirt, and desert boots. His biceps and triceps strained the short sleeves of his shirt. Without the baseball cap, this time I knew that I was looking at Bernardo O'Reilly. Even with the gray in his beard, his thick tousled hair made him look younger than when I first saw him.

Without a word, he sat on the bench beside Maria Tolsa so that they were facing in opposite directions. She stopped combing her hair and put the comb on the table. They looked at each other for a moment, then reached out to each other and kissed, the long, lingering kiss of practiced lovers.

I heard Valencia's sharp intake of breath. I wrenched my eyes away from the couple in the room and glanced at him. His face was hard and his eyes were narrow and gleaming. I could still hear the music from somewhere outside, but it seemed to come from another world. It was as if everything we were and everything we would ever be was concentrated here in this place at this moment.

Maria Tolsa and Bernardo O'Reilly rose from the

bench. Hand in hand, they took the few steps to the bed, where they sat down and began kissing again, their hands roaming each others' bodies.

I quietly stepped over to Valencia.

"My friend, we've been had," I whispered. "Let's get the hell out of here."

Valencia held up one hand, still intently staring into the room.

Now the lovers were lying on the bed. They both had their shirts off and their preliminary lovemaking showed all the signs of not being preliminary much longer. Valencia looked at his watch, took a deep breath, gently parted the beads and stepped into the room. I couldn't believe that he was going ahead with the plan, but I followed him in, my guts churning like a blender.

Valencia brought his Glock down hard on the back of O'Reilly's head. Maria Tolsa jerked upright, took us in with wide dark eyes, and opened her mouth to scream.

If she screamed, no one heard it because the next sound was an explosion that rocked the building. Lilly and Nicole were right on time.

CHAPTER 29

VALENCIA GRABBED Maria Tolsa's wrist and she reared back and slapped him hard in the face with her other hand. From the feral look on his face, I was afraid that he might kill her. It would never do for the hostage to be done in by her rescuers, so I grabbed her shoulder, yanked her around so that she faced me, and pressed my SIG hard against the unconscious O'Reilly's head.

"I know that you understand English," I said. "If you give us any more trouble, I blow his brains out. Understand?"

"*Si,*" she replied, all the starch gone for now, "I understand."

I wasn't about to commit murder. At least I didn't think so. But for all she knew I was the most blood thirsty creature since Count Dracula. She was frightened; not for herself, but for the man who was supposed to have kidnapped her and was lying unconscious and bleeding across her bed.

"Please don't hurt him." Her voice trembled as she crossed her arms across her chest to hide her naked breasts. "I will do anything you say."

Valencia scooped up her blouse and a pair of white

slip-on sneakers from beside the bed and tossed them at her feet.

"*Puesto les encendido,*" he ordered.

Though it was a little late for modesty, she turned so that her back was to us and quickly slipped the blouse over her head. Holding my shoulder for balance, she pulled the sneakers onto her feet and we left the room, with me pulling her along by the wrist. We were halfway down the stairs when another explosion shook the building and nearly threw us to the cement floor below.

We'd almost reached the back door when a shirtless, black-bearded man with a big soft belly and enough body hair to weave a rug charged through the doorway on the other side of the room. He was armed, but his weapon was still in his waistband. Seeing us, his mouth fell open and it took a second for him to take everything in. Valencia was faster. He aimed the Glock and pulled the trigger, but nothing happened.

When fat boy saw Valencia raise the Glock, he dove to one side, rolled through the motion, scrambled to his feet, and reached for his weapon. He was surprisingly agile for such a big man, but he'd missed too many aerobics classes and his soft gut made it hard to get his gun out of his waistband as quickly as he needed to keep from getting shot.

I drew my SIG and fired twice, keeping my aim low. I didn't want to kill him unless I had to. I just wanted to put him out of action.

At least one shot was good, maybe both. Fat boy's right leg jerked out from under him and he hit the floor face first with an audible splat. If he tried to get back up we didn't know it because by then we were out the back door and running like hell.

As the three of us ran toward the dry river bed, there was another explosion in the plaza. Lilly and Nicole were

still on the job. We heard the chatter of gunfire, too, probably from the AK-47s, but it had a scattered and uncertain feel, as if whoever was shooting wasn't sure what
they were trying to hit or even where the target was. With
luck, O'Reilly's gang might have confused my two shots
with the shots of their own. The fact that their leader was
missing wouldn't help either.

As if to confirm my thoughts, I heard someone
scream, *"De donde el infierno esta viniendo?"* Another man
yelled, *"Tres hombres abajo!"*

Good. Wherever they were, Lilly and Nicole were still
hidden. In addition to what vehicles they damaged,
they'd also killed or wounded three men. Keep it up,
ladies. With our two, that was five down.

Now that we were out of the building, Maria Tolsa
became difficult to control. Knowing that we weren't
about to go back in and shoot her lover, she dug in her
heels and ferociously yanked at my grip on her wrist. We
had no time for this nonsense. I holstered my SIG and
clouted her on the jaw with my fist. I probably didn't hit
her hard enough to knock her out, but I certainly stunned
her. I threw her across my shoulder and we continued
our run toward the dry river bed.

I was straining and winded by the time we got there.
It felt like my legs, shoulder, and lungs were on fire.
Maria Tolsa probably weighed only one hundred and
fifteen pounds, but it was a lot more weight than I was
used to carrying for long distances while running for my
life.

We slid down the side of the river bank in a hail of
gravel and loose soil. I dumped her on the ground and
collapsed, gasping like Doc Holliday on his death bed.
Her head lolled back and she muttered something that
didn't sound complimentary. As I expected, she was
stunned but not unconscious. She was coming out of it

fast, too. There was a fourth explosion while we were running to the river bed and a fire was blazing in the plaza around the dry fountain. We could see the flames over the top of the buildings.

While I struggled to regain my wind, after a long look back the way we'd come, Valencia announced, "It looks like no one's after us, at least not yet."

"That won't last long once they find O'Reilly," I gasped. "It's a good thing they don't know which way to go. What's wrong with your Glock?"

Valencia took it out and examined it.

"Don't know. Maybe I damaged it when I hit O'Reilly."

"The guy must have a helluva hard head. Here, take my Colt." I handed it over. "The extra clip, too."

The good news was that I'd packed a backup. The bad news was that our armament was badly reduced. With the two shots I'd fired, we were down to twelve rounds and two clips.

"Are you ready?" Valencia asked.

"Hell no," I replied, my chest still heaving.

Valencia grinned. "Time to go anyway."

We started down the river bed toward the jeep. Maria Tolsa's legs were still rubbery so I threw her over my shoulder again. This time I got about five hundred yards before I had to take another break. Valencia took a turn, but although he was strong for his size he was too small to carry very far a woman who only weighed about forty pounds less than he did.

After I took another turn, she was able to walk, although she was still shaky. Even with that, once she was on foot our progress was a lot faster. As we neared the spot where we left the jeep, we stopped so that Valencia could slip up to the rim and take another look. There hadn't been any more explosions and by now the

gang must have discovered that their leader was unconscious and their hostage missing.

Valencia scrambled down from the rim. I could see the
urgency in his movements.

"Someone's out there, moving very cautiously. I can't
tell how many. I didn't hear a vehicle, but they may have
one coming up."

The long head start we'd hoped for was already shot
to hell. We always knew that Lilly and Nicole couldn't
disable all their vehicles. Now our only hope was that
what vehicles survived were still back at the complex,
and even then it was going to be close.

I pulled Maria Tolsa to her feet.

"How the hell did they know to come this way?" I
asked.

There was something about the woman's body
language that made Valencia take a good hard look at her
as we started moving.

"Look at her feet," he said.

Without breaking stride, I looked down. She was
running barefoot. She'd kicked off her shoes without our
noticing and gave O'Reilly's gang a dandy little trail to
follow. Although her feet were cut and bloody from the
rough ground, she never cried out because she didn't
want to warn us. Whatever she was – and quite a few
things came to mind – she was tough and smart. She was
also smirking. We saw it even in the dim light.

"Perra!" Valencia snarled.

She replied to being called a bitch by spitting on the
ground at his feet.

It only took a few more minutes to get to the jeep,
although it seemed like a couple of hours. When Maria
Tolsa started to climb in I gave her shapely butt a healthy
shove that propelled her headlong into the back seat. I

got in on the passenger's side while Valencia eased behind the wheel and started the engine.

A second before the ancient engine came to life my stomach jumped when I heard the sound of another engine in the distance.

They were after us, and close enough that we could hear them.

CHAPTER 30

It was possible that they didn't know the turf as well as we did. Given how sloppy they were about security, they may not have conducted even a rudimentary exploration of the area. On the other hand, they could use their headlights and we couldn't because it would give away our position.

Either way, our hoped-for head start was down to almost nothing and we were barely underway. We hadn't counted on a hostage who didn't want to be rescued. Finding Maria Tolsa with O'Reilly slowed us down and then the trail she left with her shoes gave us away.

As much as I didn't like it, I couldn't think of an alternative to what I was about to propose. I leaned toward Valencia as we bumped and crashed along the river bed because I didn't want the woman in the backseat to hear me.

"When we get to a good spot, slow down a little so I can jump out," I said. "I'll meet you back at camp."

I swayed in my seat as Valencia downshifted and turned the wheel violently to the right to avoid a gaping hole in the river bed. Once he had us moving safely forward again he shook his head.

"Don't be crazy," he said. "You'll never make it."

"We don't have a choice," I said. "It's got to be me. You have the language and know the area better than I do. If I can distract 'em and maybe send 'em off in another direction I'll make my own way back to camp or call you on my cell phone."

We bumped wildly along, with Valencia spinning the steering wheel left, right, and left again.

"Do you want your weapon back?" he asked, squinting into the darkness.

"No, keep it," I replied. "You might need it."

"Take the glasses, at least."

Using his right hand, he lifted the night glasses over his head and handed them to me. I slipped the strap over my head.

I checked my SIG and made sure that I still had the extra clip in my hip pocket. At the next relatively smooth spot, Valencia slowed down. I took a deep breath and jumped out of the jeep. I staggered and went to my knees when I hit the uneven ground, but got to my feet and quickly scrambled out of the river bed.

Now what? What I'd left unspoken was *how* I was going to distract our pursuers, mostly because I didn't know. There wasn't much time to think about it as I ran back the way we came at a half crouch. It wasn't long before I saw their headlights bouncing along the river bed.

Fortunately I hadn't gone far when I found what I wanted; a waist-high rock on the rim that might conceal my gun flash. Shooting down would be an advantage, too. I knelt beside the rock and waited for the SUV to come within range. I had no idea how many of O'Reilly's men were inside, but at this point it didn't matter. I was committed.

Down on one knee, I sighted along the side of the

rock, aiming at the SUV's grill. I wanted to make as much racket as possible. It would be nice to hit the windshield and maybe shatter it all to hell, but I couldn't risk aiming at it because with the night and the way the SUV was bouncing around the shot was too difficult from this position. If I missed altogether, with all the noise they were making they might not even notice they were under fire. At least if I missed the grill I'd probably still hit something and maybe even do some damage to the engine.

I squeezed the trigger and took out the SUV's left headlight. I took off running as soon as I fired, staying parallel to the river bed. I wanted to get behind them for another shot. That way maybe they'd think I was more than one guy.

My first shot had the desired effect. The SUV's remaining headlight and engine shut off. I heard the occupants pile out. A lot of excited Spanish flew through the air, too, but they were talking too fast and I was running too hard to make any sense of it.

When I figured that I'd gone far enough, I peered over the rim into the riverbed. I was about three-quarters of the way in back of the SUV, on its right side. I saw four men, one standing on each side of the SUV and two in front. The two in front were moving forward very slowly. O'Reilly was at the driver's side door. Everybody had their weapons out, including what looked like AK 47s carried by the men in front.

I aimed at the man standing on my side and pulled the trigger. I was too far away and it was too dark to be sure of my shot. Without hanging around to see if I hit him, I went over the rim and into the river bed in back of the SUV. I snapped off another shot as I ran and scrabbled back up on the other side.

Automatic weapons fire blasted to the right and to the rear of the SUV until a deep authoritative voice bellowed,

"Pare el encender, usted los idiotas! You no puede incluso ver en lo que el su tirar!"

Since enticing them to shoot wildly at nothing was my plan, I was pleased to hear that I was so successful, although I would have liked it a lot better if O'Reilly wasn't so good at keeping his men under control.

Now I was on their left, down to three shots and one clip. All four men were still standing. I wasn't surprised that I missed the man I'd shot at. It would have been blind luck if I'd hit him and I'd already used up all the luck I could hope for by taking out the headlight.

In the silence, I realized that I couldn't hear the engine from our old rattletrap. Good. Valencia had the sense to keep going even if he heard the shots. He was gaining ground while they stayed behind to deal with me.

I peered through the night glasses. The men in front had stopped moving, and all four were crouched on the ground as if they weren't sure what to do next. O'Reilly was shielded from the front by the open driver's side door, but he wasn't shielded from me. He called out to the men in front to come back to the SUV so they could get going.

"Pienso que hay solamente un asshole hacia fuera allí de todos modos," he yelled.

"We'll see who the asshole is, pal." I carefully sighted right in the middle of O'Reilly's chest. But just as I squeezed the trigger, he stepped into the driver's seat and the shot clanged harmlessly off the SUV's frame with a shower of sparks.

O'Reilly jumped out of the SUV and ran toward me with an incoherent scream, blasting away as he ran. The other three followed, all of them firing their weapons haphazardly. I was pretty sure that I hadn't been seen, but O'Reilly somehow sensed the direction of the shot. The others were just following their leader.

This was no time to stand and fight. I took off like a jack rabbit, this time headed toward the front of the SUV. By the time O'Reilly and his men came out of the river bed at my old position, I was out of sight in the darkness.

Breathing hard, I flattened myself on the ground and looked through the glasses. They'd found nothing but frustration and were headed back to the SUV. Their heads twisted and turned as they walked, wondering where the next shot might come from. Good. I had them rattled.

If they played it smart and didn't let adrenalin get the better of them, they'd ignore me and continue the pursuit. But it's hard to ignore someone who's shooting at you, even if, as O'Reilly said, you're pretty sure it's just one asshole.

I slithered into the river bed on my belly and found a depression in the ground on the left side. I knew from experience that the other side was virtually impassible at this point, so the SUV would have to pass within a short distance of my hiding place. It was a chance for me to get off at least a couple of close-range shots, especially since I knew they wouldn't be moving very fast.

It was a lot closer than I thought. For a second I was afraid that the SUV was going to run right over me. Just as it flashed through my mind that I'd waited too long, the SUV veered off with only a few feet to spare. As it passed, I aimed through the open window at the man in the front passenger's seat, fired twice, and a high-pitched scream told me that I hit him.

The SUV swerved sharply away from me and stopped as I took off again, this time up and over the rim. I paused for a second at the top and looked back. I wanted them to chase me and the only way they could do that was if they saw me. To get their attention, I fired another shot and the bullet clanged off the SUV.

Faster than I thought possible, the SUV wheeled

around, nearly tipped over, barreled over the top of the rim like an angry dinosaur, and came straight at me with its single headlight piercing the darkness.

I ran until I thought my heart would burst. Now that I was away from the river bed, there were fewer places to hide. I dodged to the left and hit the ground, counting on the night and my dark clothes to keep me hidden. Lying on my belly and gasping for air, I ejected my empty clip and replaced it with the only one I had left. I was down to eight shots.

The SUV moved in a wild zigzag, hoping to pick me up with its headlight. Someone was also using a bright hand-held spotlight as they leaned out of the window and the combination was more effective and covered more area than if they had two headlights. If they continued in this direction and I stayed where I was they'd find me pretty quickly.

I got to my feet and started running, but didn't get far before the spotlight found me. Fortunately, it was hard to keep it focused from a bouncing SUV. I eluded the light and circled back. Assuming that I was running away from, and not toward, my pursuers, the spotlight probed past me, its beam knifing through the desert night.

As the SUV rumbled past, I fired at the spotlight, thought I heard a yell, and started running again. By now I was in a bad way. My breath was coming in hard rasps, my legs were heavy, and there was a sharp pain in my chest that wouldn't go away. I couldn't keep this up much longer.

Without slowing down, the SUV made a one hundred eighty degree turn that was so sharp it nearly rolled over again. One of the AK 47s rattled and the shots kicked up sand to my left. I didn't know if they were lucky or if they'd spotted me. I turned to the right and when the SUV swerved to the right the spotlight captured me.

I jumped into a shallow gully as the spotlight seared the air over my head. When the SUV was close enough, I fired two more shots that ricocheted off the front. For all the effect it had I might as well have thrown rocks.

The SUV was bearing down fast so I got up and started my labored zigzag running again. My legs felt like lead and every breath was torture. Leaving the river bed for open country was a really dumb idea, and I knew that I'd come to the end of the line.

I was trapped in the SUV's lights and couldn't move fast enough to elude them. As it closed in, I knelt on one knee and fired two rounds. The roar of the engine seemed to fill the universe and the glare of the lights made it seem as if the whole world was on fire.

Suddenly there was another, even louder, sound to my left. Two blazing headlights blinded me and I threw my left arm up to shield my eyes.

All I could see behind the lights was a huge formless beast that was making an incredible amount of noise and moving like a tank at warp speed. If there was ever any doubt about it, the reinforcements meant that I was done for.

Would they kill me here or kill me later? Probably later, I figured. They'd want me to talk first.

And then the monster smashed into the front quarter of the SUV, a glancing blow that brushed the SUV out of the way like a toy kicked by a giant. I was so stunned that I just stood there. I couldn't run and I didn't have anywhere to hide even if I did. The thing turned and rolled to a sliding stop between me and the damaged SUV. Still blinded and half deaf, I heard Lilly's voice. "Jump up here, quick!"

I ran forward, bumped into the side of the big Dodge Ram, and felt Lilly's hands grab my arm and pull me up. I fell into the truck bed with a force that knocked the wind out of me. I heard Lilly shout, "We've got him! Go! Go!" and the big truck rumbled away.

"Stay down!" Lilly ordered. Since my back hurt and I was having trouble breathing, I didn't have much choice.

Lilly got to her feet, her backside braced against the back of the cab for balance, and hefted the grenade launcher to her shoulder. The SUV was badly crinkled on the right front quarter, but it was still on the chase and bumping after us like hell, its single headlight illuminating the truck in the night.

"Okay, stop!" she shouted. The truck stopped so quickly that I slid all the way to the rear of the truck bed and cracked my back again.

Lilly took aim with the grenade launcher and let it rip. It wasn't a perfect shot. It's not easy to shoot something that's coming directly at you. She'd over-compensated and hit the ground in front of the hard-charging SUV, but the concussion stalled the engine and blew out both front tires.

As we pulled away, the last sound I heard from the SUV was O'Reilly cursing as he frantically tried to restart the engine while someone fired his AK 47 harmlessly into the darkness.

That, and Lilly shouting, "Up yours!"

CHAPTER 31

WHEN WE ROLLED BACK into camp I carefully climbed out of the back of the truck and took inventory of my parts to see if they were still in working order. Fortunately, all I found was a few scrapes and bruises to go with a sore back.

Assured by Valencia that everything was under control and we weren't going anywhere, I staggered into the camper and flopped down on the sofa bed without bothering to unfold it or even take off my filthy clothes. I went to sleep almost instantly, but not before exchanging glances with Maria Tolsa, who was lying on the bed in the next room, one wrist handcuffed to the head board.

I woke up very slowly, inch by inch. The warm sunlight shone through the window above my head and bathed the inside of the trailer in a rich golden glow that reminded me of the Joni Mitchell song "Chelsea Morning," where the sun poured through a window like butterscotch. I didn't know how long I'd been asleep, but it had been a while.

Even so, I didn't want to get up. Luxuriating somewhere in that blissful state between wakefulness and sleep, it was almost as if I'd dreamed the whole thing: the kidnapping; Valencia; *El Campeador*; Lilly and Nicole; the meeting with Jorge Tolsa; La Paz; and everything that happened last night - especially everything that happened last night. I had the wonderful feeling that I was still dreaming, and when I finally woke up it would be at home in my own bed, with Dina on one side and Brewster on the other. I held on to that feeling for as long as I could before grim reality intruded in the form of Lilly's blonde head poking through the camper's open door and asking if I wanted coffee and breakfast.

"Mmmm," I replied, my voice thick with sleep. "I didn't know this establishment had room service."

"It doesn't," she said with mock severity. "This is a one-time exception. I'd advise you to take advantage of it while you can."

"As long as you put it that way, the answer is yes, you silver-tongued devil," I said.

After a hot shower and shave, three cups of coffee, orange juice, four scrambled eggs, about a pound of bacon, and an English muffin slathered in butter, I felt more or less human by the time I joined Valencia, Lilly, and Nicole outside around the table. My back where I dinged it in the truck was sore, and I moved like an arthritic old man, but it wasn't the kind of deep pain that told me it was something to worry about.

It was a beautiful day everywhere I looked, with blue sky, bright sun, glistening ocean, and bright sandy beach all around me. After what almost happened last night, I had the feeling that Devil's Island probably would have looked pretty good this morning.

Maria Tolsa was sitting in a lawn chair firmly sandwiched between Valencia and Lilly. With my usual keen eye for detail, I noticed that her right wrist was handcuffed to the arm of the chair. It wasn't heavy, but if she tried to run she wouldn't move very fast with a lawn chair attached to her wrist. Her long black hair was gathered behind her neck with a silver and turquoise beret. She was wearing a white short-sleeved blouse and dark blue knee-length shorts that I recognized as belonging to Nicole, except that they looked better on her, and that was saying something because Nicole was an attractive woman.

Despite the fact that her dark eyes radiated hot anger mixed with scorn, which is not the most appealing of attitudes, Maria Tolsa exuded the most powerful sex appeal I'd ever experienced. It was an aura redolent of sex in beds, sex in elevators, sex outdoors, sex indoors, sex on beaches, in backseats, on floors, on kitchen tables, on land, sea, and in the air, the kind of reckless sex that would drive a man to take all the risks there were and the consequences be damned, if he even thought of the consequences. Whether that aura had any staying power I didn't know. Valencia seemed immune to it, but maybe he was working like hell to seem to be immune to it. There was at least one man who *had* risked everything for her, and that was Bernardo O'Reilly.

Tearing my eyes away from our captive, if a captive is what she was, I grinned at Nicole and Lilly.

"You two don't follow orders very well, do you?"

"Would you rather we'd left you out there in the desert?" Nicole's eyebrows rose nearly to her hairline. "I seem to recall that you were about to become a hood ornament when we showed up to save your sorry ass."

"I said you're not very good at following orders," I replied. "I never said it was a bad thing."

I twisted one way, and then the other, until my neck gave a sharp and satisfying crack.

"Do you think they can ID the truck?" I asked.

"I doubt it," Nicole replied. "Everything happened pretty fast, and in the dark one truck looks pretty much like another. I bet they were even more surprised than you were."

"In that case, they were *real* surprised," I admitted. "Was there any damage?"

"A few scratches," she replied. "If you didn't know they were there, you wouldn't even notice 'em. We got 'em on our front bumper. You've probably got more dings than the truck."

"What about the license plate?" I asked. "Think they saw it?"

"We took it off before we got there," answered Lilly.

"You seem to have thought of everything." I raised my coffee cup in a toast. "Here's to being rescued in the nick of time, and may it never be necessary again. Now would somebody please tell me exactly what happened last night?"

Valencia took the lead.

"When I got back here with the woman, there was no one around," he said. "Of course, I did not expect to see you yet, but I was afraid that these two had been killed or captured. There was no way to tell. I could not leave the woman alone, so I did the only thing I could do; I handcuffed her inside the trailer and waited."

Knowing Valencia, it was significant that he refused to call Maria Tolsa by her name. He spit out "the woman" like it was a curse, or something he'd scrape off his shoe.

Lilly and Nicole looked at each other.

"You start," said Lilly.

"It went almost perfectly at our end," Nicole said. "The only problem is that one of the grenades was a dud."

"The long gap between the first and second rounds," I said.

Nicole nodded. "We took out three or four vehicles and several of the gang. They never did figure out where the fire was coming from. The poor bastards ran around like crazy. They didn't know whether to shit or go blind."

"Colorful," I said. "Your description is very colorful."

"It's her influence." She jerked her head toward Lilly. "I didn't talk like that until we started working together. Anyway, we kept one grenade in reserve, just in case, and pulled out just like we planned."

"Well, maybe not quite like we planned," Lilly added. "The thing is, we didn't get all the vehicles and we knew it. We didn't have enough grenades for that, and they were too spread out anyway. So instead of pulling out and coming back here like we were supposed to, we decided to hang back and swing over to the other side of the river bed to see if anybody went after you, and you got the kind of head start you needed. We saw the white SUV take off on your trail like a bat out of hell. They didn't even hesitate. We were pretty surprised at that. I mean, how did they know which way to go?"

"I already told them about Cinderella and her glass sneakers," Valencia interrupted, glancing at "the woman," who responded with a grim little smirk.

"We knew you didn't have much of a head start," Lilly continued. "So …."

"… we followed at a distance, staying away from the riverbed so they wouldn't spot us," interrupted Nicole. "When we heard the shots we knew that something had gone really wrong. We got as close as we could without giving our position away. Then Lilly moved in on foot until she saw you doing your Rambo routine. When she didn't see Valencia and our jeep anywhere, it was pretty obvious what was going on. You looked like you could use some help, and, well, you know the rest."

It was close. Much too close. Just thinking about it made me shudder. Lilly saw my reaction, reached across the table and patted my hand. Suddenly aware of what she was doing, and that Nicole and Valencia were watching with vast amusement, she jerked back her hand like she'd touched a hot stove. Nicole and Valencia grinned while Lilly looked sheepish. I tried to appear to be above it all, but I don't think I succeeded.

After talking through last night from my point of view, I had one question: "Now what?"

"We wait," Valencia said.

"Wait?" I asked. "Why? For what?"

"While you were sleeping Lilly and Nicole checked out the airport," he explained. "What they took to be O'Reilly's men - anyone who looked out of place and didn't seem to be doing anything in particular; watching rather than waiting - were all over. When they returned I drove to the marina. It was the same thing; crawling with O'Reilly's men. We'd never get her out either way without trouble. I'm sure they're watching the roads, too, since that's the most obvious way to get back to Cabo San Lucas. There aren't many roads we can use and they know it. And don't forget that they have the police, at least some of the police, on their side."

"That's a lot of manpower," I said. "I think I'm impressed. Just how many men do you think O'Reilly has?"

"Apparently as many as he needs," replied Valencia.

"And we can't go to the La Paz cops because we don't know who's in O'Reilly's pocket," I said. "Plus, if we contact Tolsa and *he* goes to the cops chances are pretty good the locals will get wind of it somehow. And maybe Tolsa's phones aren't secure? Who know who might be listening? Could be the good guys, could be the bad guys. The problem is that we don't know which is which."

I shook my head. "Things just get better and better, don't they?"

"You could put it that way," Valencia said. "Now that

we have the woman, they'll expect us to run for it. I believe that we should wait here for a while and …"

"You will not succeed. You never had a chance. You are fools, all of you."

As far as I knew, those were the first words Maria Tolsa had spoken since she promised to be good or I'd shoot O'Reilly. Her voice was low and surprisingly soft, considering that she'd threatened us and called us fools.

Valencia looked like he wanted to belt her. Nicole and Lilly just laughed.

"So what's your story?" I asked. "How did the damsel in distress turned out to be a dragon?"

She raised her wrist as far as the handcuffs would allow.

"Let me out of these and I will tell you everything."

Lilly, Nicole, Valencia and I looked at each other, waiting for someone to say something.

"What's the matter? Are you afraid?" she sneered. "The four of you afraid of one woman?"

"I'm for taking the cuffs off.," I said. "I don't see a downside. There's four of us and one of her. The only thing she could do is run. She wouldn't get very far and she knows it. I say turn her loose. Anything she has to say might be helpful, and it'll be interesting to hear it at the very least."

Lilly and Nicole nodded their agreement. Valencia didn't like the idea, but the desire to hear what she had to say was too strong.

Valencia took the key out of his pocket and removed the cuffs. Maria Tolsa did what everybody does when they're released from handcuffs, no matter whether it's been ten days or ten minutes; she vigorously rubbed her wrist.

"Okay," I said. "Start talking."

CHAPTER 32

MARIA TOLSA LOOKED around the table from one face to the next, as if she was taking our measure. As I'd noticed before, she wasn't at all intimidated, or, if she was, she hid it well.

Not for the first time, I was struck by the almost ridiculous peculiarity of the situation. What bizarre convergence of events conspired to deliver me to this place at this time with these people to do what we were doing? The kidnapped woman we had risked our lives to rescue was about to tell us why what we thought we knew couldn't be more wrong while we sat on a beautiful beach in La Paz, Mexico, and calmly listened as if we did this kind of thing every day.

"What do you know about Jorge Tolsa?" she asked.

"We know that you are his wife and he wants you back," Valencia answered. "We know that you were taken from his home - from *your* home - to be returned for a large ransom. We know that we were sent to bring you back and here you are. And we know that you are going back."

She tossed her head, as if to get a lock of hair out of

her eyes, except that there was no such lock of hair. The movement was one hundred percent disdain.

"You are doing this for money," she sniffed.

"Of course, we're doing it for money," I snapped, already tired of her attitude. "It looks to me that you're doing whatever you're doing for money, too. You're in no position to look down your pretty little nose at us or anyone."

"You don't understand!"

She pounded the table with her fist, consumed by impatience and frustration, like a teacher trying to break through to a group of exceptionally dull students.

"I'll ask you again, what do you *really* know of Tolsa?"

We didn't say anything. There was no need. She was about to answer her own question.

"My family was poor," she continued. "My father operated a fishing boat. It was one of the Tolsa fleet. For working like a slave twelve hours a day seven days a week, he was paid the equivalent of twenty dollars a day. He wasn't even supposed to keep the tips from his customers, although he did sometimes keep a few dollars for himself. Why shouldn't he? He had to support my mother, my sisters, and my brothers."

She coughed into her hand.

"May I have something to drink?"

"What would you like?" I said.

"Water or a soft drink, if you have it."

I went to the little refrigerator inside the camper. I put some ice in a glass and brought the glass and a can of diet Pepsi to the table. Maria Tolsa cleared her throat, poured the Pepsi into the glass, and took a long deep drink, draining half the glass.

"From the time I was little more than a child, Tolsa would come to our home," she continued, the fingers from both hands entwined around the glass. "He said it was to talk to my father. But he didn't do this with any of the other captains. It was me. I sensed it even then, even if I was too young to know. I could feel his eyes follow me everywhere I went. He wanted me from the first day he saw me."

"Eventually my father arranged to buy his boat from Tolsa, who also paid to set him up with everything he needed to run a fishing business. He still worked for Tolsa, but as an independent contractor. He even agreed to buy for our little house, too, with the agreement that my father would pay him back over time."

"But two years later my father was badly injured in an accident and lost a leg. There is not much use for a crippled fishing boat captain. There was no insurance, but Tolsa promised that he would be loyal to my father the same way my father was loyal to him for so many years. It wasn't long before he changed and went back on what he promised. He said it was just business, but I know now that he planned it from the beginning. If there hadn't been an accident, Tolsa would have found another way to get what he wanted. My father signed things that he did not understand. The interest on the loans for the boat and the house was more than twenty percent. Tolsa was my father's *patron* and he promised us his protection, but that promise was never written on paper and no lawyer ever saw it, so as far as Tolsa was concerned it did not exist. My father is uneducated and naïve. When Tolsa made his promises, he believed him. As usual, the law was on Tolsa's side. The law is always on the side of people like him; the wealthy, the powerful, the unprincipled."

She looked at each of us in turn to gauge the effect of her story. Seeing neither encouragement nor discouragement, she continued.

"Of course, I did not know all of this until later. My father kept it to himself because he believed that keeping trouble to himself is what a man does. In his way, he was trying to protect his family."

"By this time, I was attending the university here in La Paz. I was the first of my family to go to university. You Americans, and perhaps even you" – she lifted her proud chin at Valencia - "don't know how much that means to a poor family in Mexico. I did not know it, but Tolsa paid for the university, too. I think he knew that it was best to have me out of the way when he trapped my family in his net."

"By now, counting the interest my father owed Tolsa more than two million pesos. He tried to sell the boat but no one would buy it because Tolsa made it clear that no one should make an offer. He offered to sell the boat back to Tolsa, but Tolsa only laughed and said that he did not need another fishing boat. My family was about to lose everything. It was then that Tolsa told my father that he had loved me for years. He said that if I married him he would forgive all the debt, give my father the house and the boat, and take care of my family for the rest of their lives. By then my mother was sick, too, with cancer. To you Americans, medical care seems cheap in Mexico, but it is expensive for a poor family."

This time it was me who looked at the others to see how the story was playing. A half-smile flickered around Valencia's mouth as he stared out at the ocean, looking at nothing in particular. He resembled a man who was trapped into listening to a pitch from an aluminum siding salesman. With her chin planted in her fist, Nicole seemed indifferent, as if she didn't care one way or the other. Under the gruff exterior, I knew that Lilly had a soft spot and it was showing big time. She looked like she might offer to adopt Maria Tolsa any minute.

And me? I wasn't sure how I felt. For all I knew this woman was lying through her perfect teeth and sensuous lips. Given her behavior so far, she probably was. But then again, maybe not. In Mexico, and everywhere else, stranger things have happened.

And even if her story was true, so what? Did it really change anything? The answer, as far as I could tell, was no. We weren't social workers. We had a job to do and it didn't involve sorting out a family soap opera.

"Finally my father agreed." Her eyes asked the question before anyone could voice it. "Does that seem cruel to you? Do you think it is wrong? You should understand that when my father was young many marriages were arranged, including his own. It still happens sometimes. When I found out what had been promised I tried to kill myself. I didn't see a way out. If I didn't marry Tolsa, my family was ruined. But I hated Tolsa for what he did. I told myself that I could never marry such a man."

"It was 'nardo who kept me alive, who kept me sane. We met at the university and became lovers. Like many young people, we thought that we were going to change the world. Since then, life with Tolsa has shown me how silly we were. The rich are too powerful and they will always win. But maybe, just this once, they won't. In some ways, 'nardo is like a little boy, so idealistic. In others, he inspires everyone around him."

Valencia had heard enough. He was having none of it.

"That is a nice little fairy tale," he sneered. "All it needs are a few stepsisters and an evil stepmother. But Bernardo O'Reilly is not Prince Charming, you are not Cinderella, and I am not moved to tears."

Maria Tolsa drank the rest of her Pepsi and put the glass on the table with an emphatic thump.

"All this self-righteousness is amusing, especially coming from a bought dog like you," she said, her eyes gleaming with scorn. "Tolsa bought you just like he buys everyone. That is what the rich do."

"How do you know all this?" I asked. "I can't believe that your father told you about it, not if he's the man you described."

"Tolsa bragged about it to me one night when he had too much to drink," she replied. "When his guard is down, he likes to gloat. He always has. He can't help himself. To him, I was just another acquisition and he was proud of how clever and patient he was in acquiring it."

I had nothing to say to that, and waited with the others for the rest of her story.

"I was in despair, but 'nardo promised that somehow we would be together despite Tolsa," she continued. "I didn't believe him, but he made it come true. After I married Tolsa, 'nardo went to work for him. Of course, Tolsa didn't know that we knew each other. Tolsa travels often on business and we were able to be together when he was gone."

"And so one day you put your little heads together and came up with a plan to fake a kidnapping and walk away with more than ten million dollars," I said. "That's a pretty sweet deal; bed partners *and* shakedown partners."

I thought she'd be angry but she only laughed.

"You think you know it all, don't you? You're just another American who thinks all Mexicans are for sale. Tolsa stole my life! My life! How much do you think that is worth? When this is finished 'nardo and I will go away to a place where even Tolsa can't find us. All we need is each other."

"Each other and ten million bucks," sneered Nicole. "So tell me, princess, how many men died so you two could live happily ever after?"

"The men who worked for Tolsa deserved to die," Maria Tolsa replied bitterly. "One of them saw 'nardo come into my room one night when Tolsa was away. Afterward, they confronted me. They said they would tell Tolsa everything unless I had sex with them. I know Tolsa. He would have had 'nardo killed somehow. I think Tolsa does love me in his way, at least as much as he can love anyone, but it's a very cruel way."

For the first time, her eyes dropped.

"And so I did what they wanted. But once was not enough. I should have known. They came back and back and back."

There was silence now, just the slow rolling sound of the ocean and the faint bleat of an automobile horn somewhere in the distance toward La Paz.

"When 'nardo found out he wanted to kill them with his own hands, but that would have ruined our plan. We had been working on this for a year. He thought of another way. You see, the guard schedules change every week. At 'nardo's suggestion, with time and patience I was able to arrange it so the three of them were on duty the night I was to be taken. They went along with it because thought they would have me again. I convinced the pigs that I enjoyed it. Instead, 'nardo killed them all."

"Why was O'Reilly fired?" I asked.

"Tolsa suspected us," she replied. "I don't know what lies he told you, but he had no proof. Somehow he sensed it. To protect himself, and our plan, when he was fired 'nardo disappeared."

"And what about the poor bastard at the trailer park?" asked Lilly. "Don't try and tell us he was part of anything. He was just a good man who got killed because he was in the wrong place at the wrong time."

Maria Tolsa took a deep breath and let it out slowly.

She did not meet our eyes as her long fingers fiddled with the empty Pepsi can. It was her only sign of nervousness.

"That was a bad thing, a terrible thing," she admitted. "It was not supposed to happen. One of 'nardo's men was out of control. He was excited by the other deaths and shot the man before 'nardo could stop him. He is dead now, too. 'nardo killed him on the boat and his body is at the bottom of the ocean."

"That was the shot we heard from the water," Nicole said, glancing around the table.

"So that's five men dead, plus anybody we killed last night, all of it for you." I shifted my weight and threw one arm over the back of my chair. "So tell me, are you worth it? Are you *that* good in the sack?"

She threw her Pepsi can at me. Even though I was sitting directly across the table, the can flew harmlessly past my head. Maria Tolsa was beautiful, but she had a candy arm.

She jumped to her feet. At first I thought she was going to run, but she didn't.

"All right, take me back to Tolsa, if you can. But just remember that 'nardo and his men are waiting. You can't hide here forever. He'll find you. He'll never stop until he does. Even if you do take me back, that changes nothing. 'nardo is mine and I am his. No matter what Tolsa does to me, we'll never stop."

I laughed out loud. It was all too strange and theatrical to be real, yet here we were.

"From the grieving husband, to the faithful wife held at the mercy of a brutal kidnapper." I shook my head. "That's one hell of a rigged trifecta."

Valencia couldn't hold it back anymore.

"Your boyfriend is a thief and a murderer and you are a lying *puta* cheating on your husband," he said, rising to his feet. "I don't believe a word of your story, not one word. Know this and make no mistake about it, one way or another, you're going back. You're going back!"

Maria Tolsa kicked the lawn chair out of her way, marched back to the camper, climbed inside, and slammed the door as if she owned it.

CHAPTER 33

HEARING Maria Tolsa's story put Valencia in a foul mood. I didn't blame him. I wasn't feeling too good about things myself.

"I should have seen it from the beginning," he muttered, staring angrily at the camper door she'd slammed in our faces.

"Should have seen what?" Lilly asked.

"He means the kidnapping, how the more you looked at it the more it didn't seem right," I said. "I was thinking the same thing; have been for a while to tell you the truth."

There was a sour look on Valencia's face. He was disappointed with himself. I knew the feeling.

"We never really knew all the details," Nicole said. "Do you two mind telling us what you're talking about?"

"You know how it goes," I explained. "You've probably run into something like it. The details don't quite add up but you ignore it because there's no reason to think that what happened was anything other than what it seemed to be. Sometimes things just don't add up. That's life. On TV or in the movies, everything comes together by the time the credits roll. But real life isn't like that. It's messy. Not every I is dotted and T is crossed. When there are things left hanging that don't make sense it doesn't surprise you because that's the way it is sometimes. Then, later on, what really happened seems so obvious that you don't understand why you didn't see it in the first place and you feel like a damn fool."

"Okay, I'll ask again … like what?" Lilly asked. "I don't like being left in the dark. Nikky and I are as deep in this thing as you two are."

"If it had been a real kidnapping, Tolsa's men probably wouldn't have been killed," Valencia explained. "With a little caution, the kidnappers could have gotten in and out by killing only the guard at the gate, and they probably could have just incapacitated him and left him there. Why make it so obvious and noisy? With a real kidnapping, it would have been much better if no one knew that it happened for as long as possible. Think about it. With caution, it might have been hours before anyone discovered that the woman was missing, probably not until morning. Even longer, if she was in the habit of sleeping late."

"Then there's her handprint, the one they found on the dashboard of the car close to the door. It probably meant that she was sitting next to the door in the front seat. But wouldn't you'd put a kidnap victim in the back seat, with someone on either side, where she could be easily controlled?"

"She wasn't bound or gagged either," Lilly said. "I saw that in the trailer park. She was walking along like she was one of them. When you told me she'd been kidnapped I assumed she was walking that way because she didn't have any choice. I mean, hell, she couldn't exactly overpower all those guys by herself. Like you said, I didn't think anything of it at the time."

"Remember what Tolsa told us about her sleeping on

the first floor because of a fear she had about sleeping any higher?" I asked Valencia. "And how all the right doors were somehow unlocked when the kidnappers came? If that woman was ever in a collapsed building then I'm Willy Wonka."

"Yeah, she made it just as easy as she could, didn't she?" Lilly agreed. "They had enough time to plan it out. Like she said, they'd been working on it forever."

"And don't forget the save Mexico group that never existed,' I added.

"I didn't see it at all; nothing," Valencia said. "She's right. I'm a fool."

"Oh, stop beating yourself up, for Christ's sake," Nicole snapped. I got the feeling that she was copping an attitude more to help Valencia out of his funk that anything she really felt. "You didn't see it because you weren't looking for it. Like Ethan said, you didn't have a reason to believe that what happened was anything other than what it seemed to be. A rich guy like Tolsa is the perfect candidate for a kidnapping. You didn't see it because as far as you knew there wasn't anything more to see. Besides, all this crap about what somebody should have seen or known or suspected doesn't matter. The real question is what do we do now?"

"What do you mean?" Valencia asked.

"Just what I said; what do we do now?"

Valencia's body stiffened at the perceived challenge, although I was sure Nicole didn't intend it that way. And I knew what he was going to say.

"Nothing has changed," he replied. "We go through with the plan. The woman goes back. If I have to take her by myself, she goes back."

"All right," I said, "then I guess she goes back."

CHAPTER 34

AFTER RETURNING THE RENTAL CARS, we spent the next several days waiting and keeping a lookout at our little cove, where the only ways to get in were the winding dirt road from the highway or along the beach. As we did when we staked out the house in town, we divided the day into shifts to watch Maria Tolsa and keep tabs on what the opposition was up to.

Valencia and I checked the airport and the marina twice and both times it was easy to spot O'Reilly's men. We saw O'Reilly himself at the marina, hanging around like he had nothing better to do, except I could see the bulge on his left hip underneath his shirt. Even from a distance, he radiated almost frantic nervous tension, like a lion who didn't know which way to spring.

Lilly and Nicole took the truck and checked out the roads. They reported what seemed like an unusual number of police on patrol, especially on the road south to Cabo San Lucas. They were even stopped at a roadblock and the truck thoroughly searched. They waited until the shift was changed so the truck wouldn't be recognized and returned to La Paz several hours later.

It looked like O'Reilly had all the bases covered. He knew that we'd have to make our move eventually and when we did one way or another he'd find out about it.

I felt like I was going out of my mind. The days of being on edge and full of manic energy that had to be rigidly controlled while we watched the guys had given way to stultifying boredom.

From the looks of it, Lilly and Nicole weren't in any better shape than I was. They both were snappy and irritable.

It was hard to tell with Valencia. He usually let people see only what he wanted them to see, but I doubted that he was enjoying the experience either.

Most of the time we let Maria Tolsa roam free around the camp. If she tried to escape we told her that we'd keep her bound and gagged twenty four hours a day. She couldn't out run us and knew it. She slept in the camper's bedroom, with Valencia and Nicole switching to the sofa bed. Lilly slept outside in a sleeping bag on top of an air mattress while I took up my usual spot on the chaise lounge. If I ever slept in a bed again, I'd probably feel uncomfortable.

At about ten o'clock on the fourth morning, Maria Tolsa announced that she wanted to take a walk.

"Yeah, right," Lilly said sarcastically. She was sitting at the table playing solitaire. "You just toddle along. Whatever. Be sure and send us a postcard."

"It's no problem," I said. "I'll go with her."

Lilly, who'd just come in from guard duty out on the road, lowered her sunglasses on her sunburned nose and gave me a "what the hell?" look over the top.

"At least it's something to do," I explained. "I'm going stir crazy."

She shrugged her understanding.

"I hear ya. Okay, enjoy your walk."

I was wearing khaki pants and a light blue polo shirt with the shirttail hanging out to hide the gun in the holster at the small of my back. Maria wore white shorts that showed off her long and tawny legs. Her red sleeveless blouse was untucked and the top two buttons weren't buttoned. What she didn't have on was a bra. It was sufficiently distracting that as we left I almost forgot to grab the binoculars from the table.

The ocean swells were on the small side, about two feet. Banks of fluffy white clouds flitted across the bright blue sky and the sunlight changed from heavy and bright to weak and diffused and back again every time the sun went behind a cloud and then reappeared a few minutes later.

After several days of inactivity, getting away from camp and walking down the beach gave me a feeling of almost heady freedom. I felt a renewed pleasure in breathing the sea air, even if it was the same sea air I'd been breathing ever since we got to La Paz. The sand beneath my feet was no different than the sand back at the camp, but it felt softer and cleaner and fresher. I could tell by the way that Maria Tolsa practically skipped along the sand that she was affected in a similar way. so light-hearted that she seemed almost girlish.

After we'd walked far enough that the camp was out of sight she slowed down so that we were walking side by side.

"Tell me, why are you in this filthy business?" she asked. "Valencia I can understand. He is a hard man who doesn't care about anyone. But you're different. Why are you doing this?"

At first I wasn't going to answer, but I relented. Why not?

"It's simple, really," I said. "He's my friend and asked for my help. Besides, you're wrong about Valencia. He cares about a lot of things. It's just that he doesn't show it. Besides, maybe we're not as different as you think we are?"

"No, I believe that you are different," she said. "But why are you here at all? Why do you live here in Mexico? At a time when so many of my countrymen are literally dying to get into your country, you decide to leave it and come here. You're too young to be retired like the other fat Americans who move to Mexico and do nothing but play golf and drink with other Americans."

"That answer's pretty simple, too," I replied. "I like the life here and I wasn't crazy about the life there, not anymore. Besides, I'm not that young, though I appreciate the compliment."

She cocked her head in an almost painfully attractive way. I recognized it for the practiced gesture that it was, but, even so, I was all too aware of her nearness, her incredible beauty, and her overpowering sex appeal.

"It's a lot of things, and some of them probably sound silly, but they all add up, at least to me," I continued. "I don't care who wins the Super Bowl, the World Series, or even who's playing. I'm tired of craven politicians, of road rage, and of corporations who buy and sell the government and both political parties. I'm tired of trivial things and trivial people masquerading as important. I'm tired of stupid trends, of a country that preaches freedom and doesn't offer it to everybody, of the media peddling crap and playing to the lowest common denominator, and all the silly people who become famous doing silly things."

"But we have all those things in Mexico, too," she said. "They're all over the world."

"I know. It's the blight of modern life. But for some reason it's easier to ignore here," I said. "I don't know, maybe it's because Mexico isn't saturated with it yet, or maybe it's that I'm a foreigner and just don't see it the way you do. Life is simpler here, at least I find it so. The problems – the corruption, for example – don't touch me that much."

I'd been asked that question a lot and I'd given Maria Tolsa my stock answer. Everything I said was true, but it was a lot more complicated than that. I'd come here to escape a life that I had all but wrecked, even if the wreckage was mostly inside my own head. I was still fighting the same battles, but it seemed a little easier now, maybe because I didn't see reminders of it everywhere I looked. So far, Mexico was good for me and I liked the feeling.

We'd walked all the way to the end of the cove. Reluctantly, we turned around and headed back. We were still a good way from camp when I saw the tiny figure of Nicole, who had the watch, come running in. Even at this distance, I could see urgency in her movement and raised the binoculars. She said something to Valencia and pointed toward the highway. I grabbed Maria's arm above the elbow and we stopped. A half minute later, a La Paz patrol car rolled into camp and pulled up beside the trailer.

I hustled Maria over to the dune line and pushed her down to the sand where we couldn't be seen. I went down, too. I put my left hand over her mouth and my right leg over her middle and hooked her legs with mine to keep her from trying to get away. I couldn't help but notice that her skin was sensuously cool to the touch.

Holding the binoculars with my free hand, I saw Valencia talking to a couple of cops who'd gotten out of the car. I scanned the camp to see if there were any clues that might give us away. My chaise lounge was still on the beach, but so what? Nothing seemed out of order. Valencia led one of the cops into the trailer, while the other one stayed outside with Nicole and Lilly.

I felt Maria squirm beneath me, but it was not a movement to indicate that she was uncomfortable or trying to get away. It was a writhing of an entirely different kind. I tried to ignore her as I resolutely stared through the binoculars, but when she wiggled again I felt something begin to happen that I could not control, and felt flushed and warm at the same time.

Valencia and the cop came out of the trailer and talked a while longer. When the police got into their car, turned it around, and drove away, I lowered the binoculars and let my head hang. I deliberately avoided looking at the beautiful woman pinned beneath me.

"You have been away from home for a long time, haven't you?"

Her voice was soft, just as her body was soft in all the right places. I felt a little dizzy.

"It's been a while," I admitted.

My voice was hoarse. I wanted to clear my throat and stand up, but I couldn't.

No, that's not right. I didn't want to.

"You could help me," she whispered.

I'd taken my hand away from her mouth and lowered my head. Her lips brushed my ear and I could feel the warmth of her breath.

"You believe me. I can tell. There would be certain ... benefits if you helped me."

"You mean like medical and paid vacation?"

By now, my voice was practically cracking. It was like being fourteen again.

She laughed. It came from deep in her throat. It

was a flattering laugh, the kind of laugh that made a man think that he was the center of the universe, her universe. It was full of all kinds of wonderful implications and every one of them rolled through my mind.

She gently took the binoculars away and put my hand on her breast. As I'd noticed earlier, she wasn't wearing a bra. Her other hand reached underneath my shirt and roamed across my chest, stomach, and back. I closed my eyes and let the erotic feeling carry me. I was breathing harder. I felt her fingers touch me along my belt line, each one a tiny caress.

It was a moment before I was able to talk, or wanted to.

"I might say 'yes' now and 'no' later."

"No, I don't think you would do that," she whispered softly, her lips touching my ear like butterfly wings. "You're not that kind of man. I trust you."

Her body turned rigid when her fingers reached the holster at the small of my back and found it empty. The reason there was no gun in the holster was because I had it in my other hand.

I sat up and looked down at her. Lying in the sand, with her dark hair splayed out around her head and her lips apart, at that moment – at any moment - Maria Tolsa was one hell of a desirable woman.

I put the gun in my holster. She sat up and watched me do it with a look I could only describe as hungry.

"And I trust you, too," I said, lifting her to her feet.

"You go to hell!"

"Yes, ma'am," I said with a nod. "I'm on my way."

She spit at me and I felt the moisture hit my cheek. Without bothering to wipe it off, I grabbed her wrist and we walked back to camp. By the time we got there my body had settled down.

How close had I come to giving in? I liked to think not very close at all. That's what I'd like to think.

The cops told Valencia that their visit was routine. They said this place was the site of the occasional drug party and they liked to keep tabs on who, if anyone, was hanging out here. We didn't believe it, of course, but it didn't matter what we believed.

CHAPTER 35

I HAD the watch that night. I was sitting alone in the darkness with my back against a palm tree about two-thirds of the way between our campsite and the road when Valencia walked up. He moved so quietly I didn't know he was there until he was standing beside me.

"What's the matter?" I asked, rising to my feet. "Can't sleep?"

He shook his head.

"I didn't want to wake Nikky, so I decided to take a walk."

We stood in the quiet darkness of the tropical night. It was warm, but comfortable. The camp was out of sight on one side and the highway was out of sight on the other. We could hear the ocean, but couldn't see it. For the moment, we might as well have been a thousand miles away from the rest of the world and all of its troubles.

After a few minutes, I said, "You know, that's one hell of a woman we've got back there. She's tough and she's smart and she's strong and she's beautiful. I've got to admit that my opinion of O'Reilly is a lot higher than it used to be just because she feels the way she does about him. And if what she says about Tolsa is true …."

Even in the dark, I could feel Valencia's probing eyes.

"What are you saying?" he asked. "This isn't a fish we can throw back into the ocean. How do you think it would go for us if it got out that we had this woman and let her go? I don't believe her story anyway. Not one word of it. It's all too perfect. How many times do I have to say it? That woman is going back to her husband if I have to do it alone."

"Okay, forget that I mentioned it," I said. "You're probably right."

"There is no *probably* about it," he said.

"No," I said, "probably not."

CHAPTER 36

WE LEFT La Paz two days later.

Everybody agreed that enough time had passed that we could make our move, but by then we probably would have left even if we didn't think so. We were desperately eager to do something, anything at all. With a little luck, we figured that we'd get through the police check point, assuming it was still there. They'd been at it for several days and the longer they went without finding anything the sloppier and more relaxed they'd be. At least that's what we hoped. Too, as we knew from the beginning, traveling with Lilly and Nicole was good cover. We were just two couples merrily camping their way through Baja, not a particularly unusual sight, particularly in the southern half of the peninsula.

Valencia and Nicole were in the truck, with Nicole driving. Lilly and I were back in the camper with Maria Tolsa. After a trip to an electronics store in La Paz, Lilly and Nicole rigged up an intercom system between the truck cab and the camper and we communicated through it.

Before we left camp, Valencia produced a roll of duct tape, preparing to bind Maria Tolsa's ankles and wrists together and then roll tape around her body to pin her arms to her sides. After taping her mouth shut, he intended to stuff her into the storage area underneath a long bench that was used for seating at the camper's dining table, but Lilly and I talked him out of it.

"It's a long drive back to Cabo. For all we know she might suffocate in there," I objected. "Even if she didn't, we're supposed to be saving her. It'd probably be good thing to return her to her husband in some kind of reasonable shape. I know you don't like her, but there's no reason to torture the woman."

Valencia looked like he could think of a hundred reasons without trying. If anything, his obvious dislike of "the woman" had intensified during the days of inactivity since we snatched her away from O'Reilly and his gang.

"If the police stop us we'll have time to put her away," Lilly added. "I promise."

Valencia reluctantly agreed, leaving her to ride in the camper with Lilly and me.

"Thank you," a visibly relieved Maria Tolsa told Lilly after Valencia stepped out the door. "Thank you for being on my side."

"Don't get the wrong idea, princess," Lilly replied, reverting to her hard-ass persona. "I'm not on your side. You give us any trouble and I'll kick your delectable ass. I still remember what happened to the night manager and how *you* – she gave Maria Tolsa a sharp poke in the breastbone with her index finger – "were the cause of it. Maybe your story's true and maybe it's a crock of shit, but he's still dead and it didn't have to be that way. So just remember that you won't get very far relying on my good nature."

As we slowly bumped down the rutted dirt road toward the highway, Maria Tolsa took a chair at the other end of the camper, where she gazed out the window. She wasn't interested in the scenery as much as she was showing her disdain by ignoring us.

"Let her pout," Lilly said softly. "To hell with it."

"Maybe I was mistaken, but I got the impression that you believed her, sort of," I whispered.

"I kinda do, at least some of it. But I don't want her to get too comfortable, just in case. And, like I said, I'm still pissed off about the manager."

"All clear," declared Valencia as we turned from the dirt road onto the highway. His voice sounded tinny and artificial through the intercom.

After fifteen minutes, he reported that we'd passed the point where Nicole and Lilly encountered the police blockade.

Through the intercom, we heard Nicole say, "You know, this might be easier than we thought."

"Maybe," Valencia said, doubt strong in his voice. "We still have a long way to go."

A few minutes later, we heard the thin wail of a siren behind us. I ran back into the bedroom and peered between the blinds of the rear window. A patrol car was coming up fast, its light bar flashing.

"Lilly, put her away!" I shouted.

I ran up to the intercom.

"You got it?"

"Yes," Valencia replied as we lumbered to the side of the road. "How is it back there?"

"We're all right. Lilly's taking care of it now. In another minute she'll be packed away like a sardine."

Maria Tolsa didn't struggle as Lilly taped her ankles together, then her wrists, and ran several circuits of tape around her waist to pin her arms at her side. Lilly flipped up the dining table, which was attached to hinges on the wall, lifted the top off the storage area, and we gently lowered Maria Tolsa inside. There was just enough room for her to lay on her back without having to bend her knees. Just like a coffin, I thought.

"If you're lucky, this won't take too long," Lilly said, ripping off a section of tape and placing it firmly it over Maria Tolsa's mouth. "If not, tough shit."

We shut the lid, put the pad on top, lowered the table, and waited.

CHAPTER 37

I LOOKED out of the window on the side of the camper facing the highway. A cop was standing next to the truck, talking to Nicole and Valencia, who'd climbed out of the cab. Another one was standing beside the patrol car, which was parked at an angle in front of the truck. The first cop made a waving motion at the camper. Valencia nodded and they walked around the front of the truck toward the camper door on the other side, with the other cop following several steps behind.

I recognized both of them. They were two of the La Paz cops I'd seen back at O'Reilly's hideout while I spent the days watching and hiding in a cactus patch.

I opened the camper door.

"This is Officer Diaz. The police are looking for an escaped prisoner and they're checking every vehicle that leaves La Paz," Valencia said.

I knew that he was repeating the story Diaz told him in case one of the cops spoke English and wondered why Valencia didn't bother to explain to us why we'd been stopped by the police. He didn't want them to know that we damn well knew why.

I stepped aside to let Diaz in. The cop, his hooked nose and swarthy complexion revealing his Indian heritage, started poking around the camper in that seemingly aimless but expert way that all pros have. Valencia and Nicole waited outside with the other one, as anyone would who had nothing to hide. We were just four innocent tourists who were putting up with a little inconvenience in the name of law and order.

I idly reached up and hooked the fingers of one hand around the edge of an open storage shelf beside the door and about eighteen inches below the ceiling, like I was a strap-hanger on a subway. I'd stashed my gun up there. I didn't want to wear it because a pro, especially a suspicious pro, would spot the bulge in a second. I was pretty sure he wouldn't search up there because there wasn't enough room to hide an infant, much less a full-grown woman. If he did decide to take a look I'd still have time to pull my gun out of its hiding place.

Out of the corner of my eye, I saw Lilly fold her arms across her chest and put one hip against the dishwasher, where she had her weapon inside on the top shelf.

Taking his time, Diaz sauntered into the bedroom, looked around, saw nothing of interest, and ambled back into the main room. He moved with that kind of easy, slow-moving arrogance cops have when they know that you think they're a pain in the ass, but there isn't anything you can do about it.

Diaz stopped in the middle of the room and gave a final look around, including a long lingering look at Lilly that did everything but disrobe her and pissed me off more than it should have. After a shrug, he was moving toward the door when a loud suddenly erupted from where we'd hidden Maria Tolsa.

Before Diaz could react, I had my gun pointed at his

big nose from less than a foot away. Lilly had her gun out, too, covering us both from the side. Diaz was smart enough not to yell for help.

After two more frantic thumps, the noise stopped. I motioned for Diaz to turn, lean against the wall, and brace himself with his hands. He was familiar with the position, although he probably didn't have a lot of practice doing it himself. I slipped his gun out of his holster, made sure the safety was on, and handed it to Lilly. I checked him for other weapons, too, including feeling inside the top of his well-polished boots, always a dandy place to carry a hideout piece or a knife.

"He's clean," I whispered. "Stay with big nose here. I'm going outside to see what we can do about the other one."

I put my gun inside my waistband at the small of my back, opened the door, and hopped down the metal steps. I didn't know if the second cop spoke English, so I decided to take the indirect route and hope that Valencia picked up on it.

"Before these guys stopped us, the top came loose again on that storage area by the kitchen table," I told Valencia. "As long as we're stopped we might as well fix it."

Valencia said something to the cop, who was younger than Diaz. It was too fast for me to follow exactly, but the gist was that Valencia was going inside the camper to help me fix something while we were stopped, so we'd be staying here for a little while if that was okay. The cop only shrugged. If anything, he looked bored, although he eyed the door waiting for his partner to reappear.

I stepped to one side, allowing Valencia to go up the steps and into the camper, with the cop following close behind. Letting me get behind him was a mistake. When he was on the steps, I grabbed his ankles and jerked his feet out from under him. He fell heavily without a chance to protect himself and his chin hit the metal steps with a loud clunk. The blow knocked him out. I rolled him over on his stomach, disarmed him, and frisked him.

Valencia stuck his out from inside the camper.

"How is he?"

"Colder than a mackerel," I said. "There's a pretty good cut on his chin, too. He'll need stitches, but he'll be okay."

"For all we know, his jaw's broken," Valencia said.

"Well, yeah, there's that," I admitted. "Right now we need to get rid of the car."

Valencia trotted to the patrol car. It started with a roar and he drove it off the road, bumping along until he was out of sight in the rolling countryside between the highway and the ocean.

He came back a few minutes later, this time with my Colt in his hand, and stuck his head in the camper.

"*Venido con mí*," he ordered, motioning to Diaz to step outside.

"What are you doing?" I asked.

"He almost certainly reported that he was stopping us. If he doesn't clear it with the dispatcher they'll know something's wrong and police will be swarming out here," he replied. "We'll be gone by then, but this way we'll have a longer head start. Hours instead of minutes. I will tell him what to say."

Valencia grabbed the role of duct tape and headed back to where he'd hidden the patrol car, prodding Diaz along with the Colt in the small of his back.

Inside the camper, Lilly and Nicole raised the table, tossed the seating pad aside and opened the lid to the storage area. Maria Tolsa's hair and forehead were bloody where she'd banged it against the lid in her attempt to signal the cop. She must have come close to knocking herself out because she was still groggy.

Nicole reached down and ripped the tape off her mouth, which elicited a help of pain.

"Well aren't you just a clever little pain in the ass," she said.

CHAPTER 38

WE LEFT the two cops all nicely taped up in the patrol car.

"You think they'll be okay?" I asked.

"Yeah, probably, but why do you care?" Nicole asked.

It was a good question. Why would I care about two dirty cops? Call it a learning experience. Never turn your back on a gringo.

"Eventually their *compadres* will come looking for them, but I suspect that it will be most of the day before the car is found," Valencia said.

"Be kind of embarrassing for them," I said. "Probably not a great career move."

"Did they report our license number?" Nicole asked.

"Yes, but I had Diaz clear it," Valencia replied. "By the time the La Paz police figure out what happened and start looking for us we'll be back in Cabo San Lucas."

"Once we get back, then what?" Lilly asked.

Valencia didn't say anything. Neither did I. For some reason, I had a hard time seeing us turn over Maria Tolsa to her husband just like that. But I couldn't think of another alternative, or even why there should be another alternative. Whatever problems the Tolsas had was for them to solve. We were supposed to find Maria Tolsa and we did. Now we were supposed to bring her back and we were. What happens after that isn't any of our business. We didn't even know for sure that the Tolsas had problems. Maybe she lied about everything, except for that part where she faked a kidnapping tried to extort ten million dollars in the process?

Like they say, every marriage has its ups and downs.

CHAPTER 39

THE DRIVE back to Cabo San Lucas was smooth and without interruption. It didn't take long for Maria Tolsa to recover from her self-imposed battering. She went to the sink in the camper and washed the blood off her forehead. She looked good doing it, too. It was so hard not to watch her out of the corner of my eye that I stopped trying. The woman could turn dental hygiene into a wild sensual fiesta.

We had paid to keep Nicole's and Lilly's site at *El Campeador* open while we were gone. We decided to leave the truck and camper there and take the old jeep to return Maria Tolsa to her husband. That way, if somebody was looking for the truck, if, say, the license number got out despite Valencia's precautions with the La Paz police, we wouldn't get hassled. As a cop himself, even though he was out of favor Valencia probably could talk us out of trouble, but he wasn't on the best terms with certain powerful people just now so it was better not to take any chances.

We decided to leave Lilly and Nicole behind, too, although it took a lot of persuading.

"We've come this far, why shouldn't we go all the

way?" Nicole asked heatedly, with Lilly nodding in vigorous assent. "I think we've earned it."

"You've earned a lot more than that, but we need the two of you as insurance," I explained. "If there are any problems with what we did or how we did it, it would be best if you stayed clear of the mess. The other thing is that if anything goes south on this deal we might need your help and you won't be able to give it if you're in the same trouble we are."

Understanding the logic, but still not happy with it, they agreed to stay put at *El Campeador* for the time being.

We put Maria Tolsa in the back seat. Before leaving *El Campeador,* she tried to change our minds one last time.

"Please, *please!* Don't take me back to that man. I beg you."

Her dark eyes were wide and soft; her expression an exciting combination of alluring and vulnerable.

"You have no idea what he's capable of, and what my life is like with him. It's still not too late."

Despite her words, she wasn't begging. Part of me thought that she was too proud for that, or at least it pleased me to think so. The way she put it was matter of fact - the way someone might say that it looks like it might rain tomorrow - and was all the more effective for it. She was stating a simple reality that scared the hell out of her, assuming she was telling the truth. And that, as I'd learned, was a tricky assumption. I still wasn't sure about our little encounter on the beach. Did she try it because she was conniving, or because she was scared? Or both?

Valencia didn't bother to reply. I felt like one of us should say something, to at least acknowledge that she'd been heard.

"I'm sorry, but it's too late and we've come too far to let you go now," I said. "We would not flourish if they found out that we had you and let you go. We've got to see this through to the end. There isn't any other choice."

As speeches go, it wasn't exactly the Gettysburg Address. Eyes gone flinty, she sank into the jeep's grubby back seat and crossed her arms. She probably didn't really think that her last-minute plea would work, but it didn't cost her anything to try.

We made our way through the stop and go traffic of downtown Cabo San Lucas and stopped at the gate to the Tolsa compound. Although we weren't in La Paz that that long, so much had happened that it seemed like a year since I was last here.

Valencia had called ahead. The guard at the gate was expecting us and casually waved us through without bothering to leave the gatehouse.

"Things have relaxed a bit since the last time we were here," Valencia said, easing the jeep into the parking area in front of the big house.

It might have been possible for our shabby transportation to look more out of place than it did, but I doubted it. In contrast to the opulent surroundings, the old pile of junk resembled a wart on the end of Miss America's nose.

"Tolsa's orders, I bet," I suggested. "After all, we *are* the good guys and he *is* expecting us. Not to mention that we're returning his beloved wife and saving him ten million dollars in the process. All things considered, I'm surprised he didn't greet us with a mariachi band. How'd he sound when you called?"

"A little strange, but it's nothing I can explain," Valencia replied. "Perhaps it's that he was not as excited as I thought he'd be."

"How are you supposed to sound in a situation like this?" I asked. "People react to things in different ways. Don't forget, the old man's been under a terrible strain."

I took Maria Tolsa's hand to help her down from the

jeep. It might have trembled just a little. She gave me a last pleading look as we walked to the big door.

Unlike my first visit, Jorge Tolsa himself opened the door before we could knock. He was dressed the same as he was the first time I met him. Everything was the same, except that he looked old and worn and much closer to the age he really was. His movements were unnatural in some way that I couldn't put my finger on, although the strain probably had a lot to do with it. I'd seen younger people crack for less reason.

"Come in," he said, stepping to one side as we passed through the doorway. It seemed like an unemotional greeting considering who we had with us.

And that was when it hit me. I blurted it out. "The guard wasn't wearing a uniform."

Before I finished the sentence the door slammed shut to reveal Bernardo O'Reilly and a great big gun in one hand, pointed right at us.

CHAPTER 40

"YOU ARE VERY OBSERVANT," O'Reilly said.

His English was heavily accented and his voice was deep and authoritative.

"But a little slow," I said.

"That is my *buena fortuna*, isn't it?" he said, inclining his head slightly.

Up close, O'Reilly looked like the sort of scruffy but sensitive adventurer who'd lead a desperate charge against the tyrant if he wasn't off somewhere consulting with his muse and writing bad poetry. In other words, he looked the part that he played all his life. But looks can be deceiving. Maybe it *was* only a part? Based on everything I'd heard so far, beneath the dashing façade Bernardo O'Reilly might be just another crook, one who happened to be obsessed with a rich man's wife.

"What happened?" Valencia asked Tolsa, his voice harsh.

"I received a telephone call ordering me to get the ransom ready." Tolsa opened his hands at his sides to illustrate his helplessness. "I was to tell no one, not even you, *especially* not you, or Maria would die a long and painful death. The caller, who I am now sure was this man, was graphic about the details. I was surprised that he even knew about you. Naturally, I did what I was told. Then this *cerdos* appeared in my home."

"Where is the ransom?" I asked. "Do you …."

"Before we go any further, you will hand over your weapons, one at a time," ordered O'Reilly, who didn't seem to mind that Tolsa had called him a swine. Why should he? O'Reilly was the one in control. The man with the drawn gun takes the pot.

He motioned at me.

"You first. Move very slowly and use only the fingertips of your left hand."

I handed my gun over. O'Reilly put it in his waistband.

"By the way, my compliments for your actions in the river bed," he said. "A most impressive display. *Muy listo.*"

O'Reilly had the easy way of someone who knows that he has the upper hand and intends to keep it.

"Maybe I was clever, like you say, but mostly I was lucky," I said.

"Lucky, perhaps, but successful," O'Reilly said. "You forced me to make many changes that I did not wish to make. I don't even know who you are." With a nod at Tolsa, he added, "But he didn't know that when I called him and told him not to inform you."

Our mutual admiration society came to an end when O'Reilly turned his attention to Valencia.

"Now you will do the same and hand over your weapon," O'Reilly ordered. "Remember, the left hand only and move very slowly."

Valencia turned over my Colt. O'Reilly expertly hefted it in his left hand.

"This is a nice weapon," he said. "It has been a long time since I've seen one of these."

With a wave of my Colt, O'Reilly motioned for Maria Tolsa to come to his side. When she did, he handed it to her, ignoring Tolsa as if the old man had ceased to matter, which probably was the most insulting thing he could have done.

"You will cover him," O'Reilly told Maria Tolsa, nodding at me. "If he moves in a way that you don't like, if he as much as twitches and you disapprove, shoot him."

Her husband couldn't take it any more. He was practically weeping with helplessness and confusion.

"Maria, in God's name what are you doing?" he cried. "Why are you helping this man?"

I had forgotten that Tolsa didn't know everything we knew about O'Reilly and his wife. When she accepted the gun and pointed it at me – she looked pretty damned expert when she did it, too – Jorge Tolsa might have been the most surprised person in Mexico.

"Shut your foolish mouth, *viejo hombre*," O'Reilly snarled, his pretense at good manners disappearing.

"Now I have something for you," he said to Valencia. "Turn around."

For a second, I thought O'Reilly was going to shoot Valencia in the back. I tensed up, ready to jump and try to stop him, which more than likely would just get the both of us shot. Instead, O'Reilly hit Valencia on the back of the head with his gun. Valencia fell on his hands and knees. Although he didn't lose consciousness, his head was hanging so low that it almost touched the ground, as if it was too heavy to hold up.

"I owed him that," O'Reilly said.

"How do you know it wasn't me who hit you?" I asked, feeling the tension drain out by body.

"I know," O'Reilly said.

Now it was Tolsa's turn.

"Where is the ransom, old man?" O'Reilly demanded. "Where is it?"

Tolsa was stunned and frightened. He was caught in a terrifying world where all the success, power, and wealth he'd accumulated over a ruthless lifetime meant nothing. He was lost, without a point of reference or anyone or anything to cling to for help. There was nothing else for him to do but to obediently shuffle over to an ornately carved table, where he picked up a black leather case.

"Here," Tolsa said, his voice quavering and uncertain.

Valencia was right about the ransom. The briefcase probably held some combination of cash and something else that was portable and easy to sell anywhere in the world. Gems, maybe; certainly something hard to trace.

"Bring it to me, old man," O'Reilly ordered, emphasizing the words "old man."

Tolsa walked across the room, holding the briefcase against his chest with both hands. Each stiff-legged step was so slow and deliberate it was as if it took an extraordinary effort of will for him to put one foot in front of the other. Tolsa truly seemed old and feeble now, not at all like the vibrant self-assured man I met in this house not so long ago.

O'Reilly motioned again to Maria Tolsa.

"Why don't you take it, *mi corazon*?"

Without a word, she took the briefcase from her husband. She had to practically pry his long fingers loose. It wasn't that he resisted her. It was as if he'd lost the ability to move his limbs.

"Maria, please, what are you doing?" Tolsa whispered helplessly. "Why?"

If the room hadn't been so still I don't think I would have heard Tolsa speak. His wife ignored him. For all I could tell, she didn't hear.

I glanced at Valencia. He had fallen over on his side,

but there was something about his body language that made me think that he wasn't as badly hurt as he seemed. Maybe it was wishful thinking, but I had a feeling that he was conscious as I was, and waiting for a chance to make a move. I was thinking the same thing. The problem was getting that chance. Time was running out.

With my Colt in one hand and the briefcase in the other, Maria Tolsa stared at her husband, as if she was seeing him for the first time. Then she looked at O'Reilly, who smiled a smile of sweet possession.

"Now, my Maria, we will ...."

She shot him square in the chest. The Colt had a lot of stopping power and the shot knocked O'Reilly down like he'd been bashed on the breastbone by a sledgehammer.

Incredibly, he didn't stay down. Whatever he might have been, Bernardo O'Reilly was no cupcake. He rolled over, worked one knee under his body, put a hand on the floor, and struggled to his feet. He still had his weapon in his hand, but I think he'd forgotten all about it. All of his concentration was focused on getting to his feet.

He faced Maria Tolsa, bewilderment etched across his face like the cracks in a broken mirror. He reached out in a supplicating way with one hand and she shot him again. This time he seemed to crumple from within, like a building blown up from the inside. He didn't fall as much as he collapsed straight down until all of his weight was on his knees and shins, with his feet tucked beneath him and his shoulders sagging. He dropped his weapon, but that was the least of his problems. O'Reilly fell forward, put both palms on the tile, and inch by painful inch forced himself to his feet one more time. I couldn't believe what I was seeing. The effort was unimaginable.

The front of his shirt was covered with blood as he weaved like a corn stalk in a strong breeze. "Maria ...."

The name was a whispered wheeze, as if the bullet holes in his chest were slowly letting all the air out.

When she shot him again it took O'Reilly in the middle of the forehead. His head jerked and there was a shower of blood. I saw the life go out of his eyes before he toppled flat on his back, like a great tree going down. His right foot twitched in some kind of macabre, nerve-driven movement that defied the bullet in his brain. Finally, the twitching stopped.

Valencia rose to his feet like a cat, his movements as fluid as ever. There was blood on the back of his shirt collar from where O'Reilly hit him on the head.

At the same time, I stepped to one side so that I was to the left of Maria Tolsa and Valencia was on the right.

"Time to give it up, Maria," I said. "You might get one of us, but you'll never get both of us before one of us gets you. Hand over the gun."

I saw Valencia shoot a glance at Jorge Tolsa, who might as well have been statuary in his own home. There was not as much as a blink of an eye. It was as if he had gone to some far-off place in his mind and might never come back. I can't swear that he even knew what was happening.

Still holding the Colt in one hand, Maria Tolsa's eyes moved from me, to Valencia, then back to me. Something in her face told me that she'd come to a decision.

"Why in God's name would I shoot the men who rescued me?"

She spoke deliberately and unnaturally, as if reciting the lines of an unfamiliar script.

"What's wrong with you?" she asked. "The *hibrido* who kidnapped and tormented me and my poor husband is dead. It is over. Finished."

I heard the words but they didn't register right away. I

felt like I'd been whacked on the head with a rubber mallet.

What did she say? Something about the bastard who kidnapped her and tormented her "poor husband" ...." did I just hear what I think I heard?

I shook my head in an effort to clear it, as if I was the one who'd taken the blow instead of Valencia, who looked like he was in the same flummoxed state.

Maria Tolsa raised the Colt, stared at it as if she was surprised to find it in her hand, and threw it to the floor. As it skittered along the tile, she dropped the briefcase in her other hand, ran to her husband and took him in her arms, whispering all manner of endearments.

I didn't bother to try to think through a translation. By now, I was getting the drift.

CHAPTER 41

O'REILLY'S MAN OUT front was easily taken. His orders were to keep anyone else from coming into the compound and to stay there no matter what. The shots inside the house didn't budge him. He probably expected some fireworks. He was guarding the entrance like crazy when Valencia and I showed up after making sure to grab all three of the guns from inside. We'd learned that trusting Maria Tolsa was not a great idea.

Once we had the guard secure I asked Valencia how he kept from being rendered cuckoo when O'Reilly bashed him on the head.

"I guessed what was coming and went with the blow," he replied as we walked back into the big house. He stroked the back of his head with his hand and it came away bloody. "Fortunately it isn't as bad as it looks."

"You Mexicans have hard heads," I said. "What if he'd shot you instead?"

Valencia shrugged. "Then I would be dead and it wouldn't matter, would it?"

It took a while for things to sort themselves out, and there was a lot to sort out.

The La Paz police were not thrilled with Valencia, or with any of us. But there wasn't anything they could do to demonstrate their displeasure, especially when it got out that at least four of them were in cahoots with O'Reilly. There were probably more, but four was enough to get a lot of public attention as the usual low-level firings and high-level reprimands churned through the La Paz *policia*. By the time it was over, it was pretty obvious that the local citizenry shouldn't count on much in the way of inter-agency cooperation between the Cabo San Lucas and La Paz police for a very long time.

But aside from those modest *caballeros* Valencia and Cruickshank, the real hero, at least in the public mind, was Maria Tolsa, who told a tale that was remarkable for its pitch-perfect blend of outright lies leavened with enough half-truths to make it seem not only plausible, but likely.

Over time, she tweaked and embellished the details until her story was nothing less than a work of art. I admired it as such, too. It was something to behold. By the time she finished, she made Eva Peron look like Typhoid Mary. She probably could have won an election for president of Mexico, except that would have meant a step down and a really big pay cut.

What was more important to her than popular acclaim is that her husband believed every word of it. The more she talked, the more he believed it. And if a rich and influential man like Jorge Tolsa believed her, then everyone else believed her, too, or at least they damn well better act like it. There was no future in the truth, even if there had to be some who suspected what the truth might be. Jorge Tolsa was a powerful man with a long reach, and when he died his wife would be a powerful woman with a long reach, and probably an even longer memory.

Were Maria Tolsa and Bernardo O'Reilly really lovers years ago when they attended the university in La Paz?

Well, yes, they were, she admitted. You know how tempestuous young people are. O'Reilly swept her off her feet in a brief, but passionate, affair. He was an experienced man of the world and she was just a naïve fisherman's daughter. How was she to know that O'Reilly would become so obsessed with her that many years later he would go to work for her husband just so he could watch her and be near her and eventually kidnap her?

But why didn't she say anything? Why didn't she tell her husband, at least?

Because as far as she knew there was nothing to tell, she explained. Her relationship with O'Reilly was the same as it was with the other employees. As far as she was concerned, whatever they had died long ago. She had no idea how he felt about her, or that he was spying on her, until it was too late. She barely even noticed the man.

But what about the witnesses, the members of O'Reilly's gang who, when they were rounded up and arrested, claimed that they saw the two of them being a whole friendlier and more intimate than is probably normal between kidnapper and kidnapee?

In short, they canoodled like crazy. What was *that* all about?

It was at this critical point that Maria Tolsa showed what she was made of. She proclaimed that she was not ashamed of anything she had to do, especially considering the circumstances in which she found herself through no fault of her own. When I read that, I could practically see that disdainful toss of her head. Magic, that's what it was.

In case there was somebody lurking in the dark recesses of Mexico who didn't get the point, she explained that she was just trying to survive, as anyone would, by doing anything she could to gain O'Reilly's trust so that she might find a way to turn the tables on him, or, at the very least, escape.

And that, if anyone failed to notice, is exactly what happened, although she modestly admitted that she couldn't have done it without these two wonderful gentlemen, plus those *gringo* women, whose names she never mentioned. After all, a woman uses what weapons are available to her in order to survive, doesn't she? And believe me, Maria Tolsa was better armed than most.

In the same circumstances, what would you have done, she asked the world? The world did not have a good answer, although the world didn't look very hard either.

So it all worked out very nicely.

The three men who discovered that Maria Tolsa and Bernardo O'Reilly were lovers when O'Reilly was employed by Jorge Tolsa were dead, killed the night of the kidnapping.

Everything else she explained away to an audience that wanted to believe her because the story was the most succulent thing they'd seen in years. Like the woman herself, it was irresistible.

Maybe Valencia and I could have blown her out of the water, but maybe not. We didn't even try.

I kept silent because Jorge Tolsa had already suffered enough. By now I was more or less convinced that her story about the dastardly web he weaved to trap her family and bring her into his bed, not to mention his cruelty during their marriage, was a lot of rot. After seeing this woman in action, it was clear that if anybody did any web weaving, it was her. Her poor crippled father and cancer-riddled mother were probably the healthiest people in Mexico.

Valencia had his own reasons for keeping silent, and whatever they were he never talked about them.

The image of the beautiful victim taking revenge on her evil kidnapper and shooting him until he was as dead as Pancho Villa was seized upon by the Mexican media, and then by media all over the world. Within a week, Maria Tolsa was a national heroine, a drop-dead gorgeous, extremely photogenic national heroine. People wanted to believe her. In some way, I think they had to believe her. In a way, it was great fun and vastly entertaining.

But did her husband *really* believe, or did he just say that to keep his dignity and his pride? I think that he did believe, mostly because he wanted to, just like everybody else.

Well, almost everybody else.

CHAPTER 42

"What a bitch!" sniffed Nicole. "I can't believe she's getting away with it."

"Men are so damn stupid," added Lilly. "A good-looking woman can get away with anything. All she has to do is wiggle her ass a little."

She winked in the general direction of the two males present, that being Valencia and me.

"Present company excepted, of course."

"When do you think she changed allegiance from O'Reilly to Tolsa?" Nicole asked.

"I think it happened just a second or two before she shot O'Reilly," I replied. "Believe it not, I saw it in her face."

"That fast, huh?" Lilly asked skeptically.

"Maybe she was thinking about it before. She probably was. But I know what I saw," I explained. "Call her what you want, but she's not indecisive, I'll give her that."

Dina and I had broken out three bottles of Dom Perignon and we were drinking it at sunset on our patio overlooking the sea; me, Dina, Valencia, Lilly and Nicole. The sun had gone down, although it was not quite dark, and a handful of the brightest stars were scattered and flickering across the sky, with the promise of more to come. Brewster was hiding in the house. For some reason, Nicole scared the hell out of him and our brave watchdog was guarding the inside of a closet. When we finished the champagne, we were going out to dinner at Villa Serena, one of our favorites. Set well back from the highway with a view to die for, lobster was the house specialty.

"But why bail on O'Reilly?" Nicole asked. "What made her change her mind after such a long time?"

Nobody had a ready answer to that one, except my brilliant wife.

"It's pretty obvious," Dina said. "You guys are just too close to see it."

"What do you mean?" Valencia asked.

"Before the kidnapping, from her point of view she had the perfect life, with her lover on the one hand and her wealthy husband on the other while she and O'Reilly worked out their plan, which probably seemed more like a fantasy than any kind of reality she might really have to actually live in," Dina explained. "But everything changed once they went through with the kidnapping and she got a good look at what life was would be like on the run."

"You mean hiding out in that lovely wreck of a resort with all those exciting companions," I said.

"Exactly."

Dina held out her glass for more champagne. Being the dutiful husband, I filled it.

"It probably sounded all right until she was confronted with what life on the run really meant," Dina continued. "She had a long delicious taste of the good life with Tolsa and when it came down to it that life was too hard to give up. Even with the ransom money, with O'Reilly she'd be on the run for the rest of her life. She was faced with the choice of life of always looking over her shoulder with good old Bernardo or wallowing in one of Mexico's greatest fortunes with an elderly husband who probably won't live much longer."

"That's true, unfortunately," I agreed. "This whole experience really aged the old man. I wouldn't be surprised if Tolsa only lasted another year or two."

"And when he goes, she no doubt inherits everything," Valencia said.

"I'd guess that she was having doubts already and probably thought about it a lot while she was with you guys, even though she continued to act like she was sticking with O'Reilly because she didn't have much choice," Dina continued. "He was the key. As long as O'Reilly was alive there wasn't anything she could do. She knew he'd keep coming and wouldn't stop. If she turned on him, he'd talk and she'd wind up with nothing and probably even some jail time. Then, when she finally got back into that big house, she got a look at how much her husband had aged, and took a final look at O'Reilly, someone who loved to play the revolutionary but never found his revolution, and someone who, in a way, never grew up, despite all his studly qualities, and she seized the moment."

"I'll say she did," Lilly said. "With both hands and that Colt."

Nobody said anything for a while. The darkness had settled in and now the sky over the ocean was awash with stars. I could hear the ocean and feel its presence without seeing it. To me, this was Cabo San Lucas at its best.

Having protected the closet long enough, Brewster came ambling out of the house and, carefully avoiding Nicole, walked over to Dina and put his head in her lap. Without thinking about it, she scratched his ears.

"What's next for you two?" I asked Nicole and Lilly.

"We're headed back home tomorrow or the next day, depending on how much we drink tonight," replied Nicole. "We're gonna take our time going back. This hadn't exactly been the most restful vacation we've ever had."

As she talked, I saw her glance at Valencia out of the corner of her eye. Their affair appeared to be over, although they probably still had feelings for each other. Like Paul Simon said in "Hearts and Bones," the arc of a love affair.

"Maybe it wasn't the most restful, but I bet it was the most lucrative," I said.

"You got that right," Lilly agreed.

Jorge Tolsa was a generous man. He paid Nicole and Lilly the same money he paid Valencia and me, and that was a lot. As a police captain, Valencia probably wasn't supposed to take it. This being Mexico, he took it anyway.

"You know, it's ironic how the truth, at least most of it, died with O'Reilly," Nicole said.

"The truth didn't die," I said, "just most of the people who could tell it."

Which gave me an idea.

CHAPTER 43

I saw Maria Tolsa four weeks later.

Her husband was in Los Angeles on business, which is why I arranged the meeting when I did. It was their first time apart since the kidnapping.

After the usual see the guard and park the car routine, I was let into the house by a staff person I hadn't seen before and escorted to the same room where I'd first met Jorge Tolsa. Maria Tolsa was even sitting in the same chair.

She rose and extended her hand. I took it and made a little bow. She looked the same and yet different. She was wearing a white linen pantsuit with red leather sandals. Her long dark hair was fastened behind her neck. She was still a hell of a desirable woman. Maybe the change had something to do with confidence? She was finally sure of her place in the world. Why shouldn't she be? As far as I knew, the major questions of her life had been settled. She'd come through the crisis and was in a much stronger position than when she entered it.

"Would you like coffee?" she asked.

"No thanks," I said.

"A drink?"

"It's too early for me," I said. "But don't let that stop you."

We stared at each other, not knowing exactly what our relationship was, or even if we had one. Were we friends? That sure as hell wasn't it. Enemies? Closer, but maybe a touch strong. I decided that it didn't matter. We didn't have to be anything.

"First I want to make it clear that neither Valencia nor anyone else knows that I've come here," I said. "If this conversation doesn't work out, it's my fault, and only my fault. If there is blame, it is mine."

She nodded, the slightest possible tilt of her head.

"Things have changed since we first met," I said. "You have become very powerful, or soon will be. If you wanted to, you could make trouble for us."

Another nod.

"But knowing what we know, we could make trouble for you, too," I added.

This time there was no nod at all. Her only reaction was her fingernails drumming on the arm of her chair. In the silence, the sound seemed louder than it really was.

She saw were I was going.

"But if we agree to say and do nothing, then there will be no trouble for anyone," she said.

"Exactly."

She rose to her feet and held out her hand. I took it and she closed her other hand over mine.

"Then let us resolve to do exactly that," she said with a bright smile.

"Yes," I agreed. "Sometimes there's a lot to be said for doing nothing."

A LOOK AT: CABO SUNSET

(CABO 3)

Private investigator mysteries aren't known for second chances —or clean exits. But in Cabo San Lucas, nothing stays buried forever.

Still grieving his wife's sudden death, Ethan Cruickshank isn't looking for work—or trouble. But when former rival Jeff LaForge, now a wealthy e-commerce mogul, claims someone wants him dead, Ethan reluctantly takes the case.

The deeper Ethan digs, the more tangled the threads become. There's LaForge's charismatic wife, Abby—Ethan's former flame and the reason LaForge never trusted him. There's the murdered photographer, Jimmy Hopper—beloved by all, except, apparently, his killer. And then there's the trio of goons who leave Ethan bloodied in a restaurant parking lot.

As old grudges resurface and bodies fall, Ethan must navigate deadly secrets, lingering guilt, and the shadows of his past. In a paradise where truth is slippery and nothing is as it seems, one question haunts him: Why did LaForge hire him at all?

With the past closing in and bodies hitting the sand, Ethan must figure out who to trust—and why LaForge hired him in the first place.

AVAILABLE SEPTEMBER 2025

ABOUT THE AUTHOR

Robert Wisehart was born in Indianapolis, Indiana, and now is fortunate enough to live in Santa Fe, New Mexico.

In between Indianapolis and Santa Fe, he worked for many years as an award-winning reporter and columnist for newspapers in Florida, North Carolina, Louisiana and Northern and Southern California, plus occasional flirtations with radio and television as an on-air commentator. Such is the changing world that three of the four newspapers no longer exist.

Later, as a freelance writer, Wisehart did everything from write speeches to ghost books. He labored as a restaurant critic and for a brief time as a one of the dreaded horde of government consultants, two words that can mean almost anything but usually add up to not much. His work has appeared in more than 200 newspapers and 30 magazines, plus several digital outlets.

Wisehart and his wife, Dana, have been married for a lifetime and intend to make it a very long lifetime indeed. They have moved much, traveled well and Dana easily is the best thing that ever happened to him. Their two sons, Marc and Carl, live in New York City.